Show Me Dirty
Sexy Stories Collection

VOLUME 3

10 EROTIC SHORT STORIES

SAGE YARBER

Show Me Dirty/ Sage Yarber. -- 1st ed.
Xplicit Press, an imprint of TLM Media LLC

ISBN-13: 978-1-62327-530-3
ISBN-10: 1-62327-530-X
eISBN: 978-1-62327-584-6

Printed in the United States of America

CONTENTS

1 SHOW ME YOUR DIRTY LAUNDRY

When the clock struck midnight, one particularly drunk frat boy hoisted a slender blonde onto his shoulders, initiating a chorus of happy birthday cheers from a crowd of partiers. She wore a happy birthday crown over her locks, which had written on it in bold permanent marker, DARLENE THE BIRTHDAY QUEEN. She rode the boy's shoulders proudly, waving her now legal shot glass with a killer grin, and splashing him with the contents every so often.

Jenna was one of the people hollering her birthday wishes at Darlene, and she ran to greet her as she clambered off of the rosy-faced boy's shoulders. It was a Sunday night, but Darlene had insisted on having her party on her actual birthday, despite the prospect of school the next morning. She wanted to spend the next day nursing a hangover as was tradition, a proud indicator of her age. Jenna was tipsy, but the exam that she would have the next day kept her from getting wasted.

"Happy birthday, cousin!" Jenna shouted with a grin. Darlene was older than her by three years, and shared her mother's side of the family.

"Twenty-one!" Darlene squealed as if she had been rehearsing the number all night. She drunkenly pressed her face close to Jenna's so that they could hear each other over the music. "I guess I gotta give you my old ID now, huh?" She batted her lashes at Jenna, twitching them into a wink. Jenna laughed.

"What would you say if I took you up on that?" she asked. She and Darlene both had small, pointed noses and round faces, but that was where their physical similarities ended. Jenna was shorter by at least three inches; her hair was her father's wavy dark brown, and her eyes were green while Darlene's were almost gray.

"No way!" Darlene giggled, and pulled Jenna into her arms. "You're just a baby, and I can't have you going to jail at eighteen! But I'll tell you what, I'll buy you drinks every so often anyway." She hugged Jenna so tightly she stumbled against her, spilling what remained of her drink down the front of Jenna's dress.

"Darlene!" Jenna gasped and pulled away from her to stare in horror at her wet dress. The drink had soaked all the way through to her bra, and she could feel it dripping down to her underwear.

"Ohhh, I'm sorry, I'm sorry!" Darlene gasped. She touched Jenna's dress, as if doing so would somehow help dry it. "I guess I'm a little drunk, don't be mad, okay?"

"Okay, fine, dammit," Jenna sighed. "I have to go soon, anyway. I have an Enviro test tomorrow." Darlene pouted up at her, whimpering a protest that Jenna could hardly hear over the music. Jenna smiled slightly. "How about you tell me how this party wraps up over lunch tomorrow?"

"If I can get up by then," Darlene said with a final sloppy wink and a kiss on the cheek. "You sure you'll be alright walking all the way back to your dorm?"

"Yeah, don't worry about me," Jenna said. Darlene's house was only a five-minute walk back to campus, and a ten-minute walk back to her dorm room. With that, Jenna gave her cousin a final wave, and headed out into the night.

The night air felt cool and prickly against Jenna's skin as she hurried through campus, especially in her wet dress. It stuck uncomfortably to her skin, and she pulled the front of her dress just a little bit so her bra could dry out. It was a futile effort. She sighed to herself and upped her pace, so that she made it back to her dorm room in record time. She was still dizzy from the drinks, and something about her situation made her giggly as she hobbled up the stairs to her room, a hot mess.

When Jenna opened the door to her room, everything looked as she had expected. Her roommate, Katie, was asleep on her bed, face down and breathing heavily into her pillow. Jenna's pile of dirty laundry was barely contained in the hamper in the corner of her own bed, just beneath her pink comforters.

Free at last, she used her phone to guide her through the dark and to her bed. She pulled off her wet dress and threw it into the laundry pile, then undid the clasp of her wet bra and threw that in as well. The last to go was her underwear. It wasn't as wet as her other articles of clothing, but it was still wet enough to be uncomfortable. She threw that in her hamper, leaving herself entirely exposed. The air conditioning had left the room cool, and she shivered, covering her still sticky body with her arms.

"Fucking punch," she muttered to herself. Jenna wasn't sure what kind of alcoholic brew her cousin had been drinking, but from the smell of it, it had been something fruity. Whatever it was, it was now sticky sweet across her breasts and down her belly. She tiptoed over to the small sink next to her closet and turned the faucet on for just long enough to soak her washcloth in warm water, and then to bring it to her naked breasts.

Jenna sighed to herself, comforted by the warm cloth as she circled one breast after the other, dabbing gently at each nipple. She went all the way down her stomach, then around the line of her panties. Satisfied, she hung the rag to dry and felt her way across the dark room to her dresser. The top drawer was for her underwear; she pulled it open and felt around. All she could feel was the smooth wood and the smooth cotton of her socks on the other side of the drawer. Had she gone through all her underwear already? Frowning, she felt for her phone and held it up for some light. The screen illuminated her drawer to reveal what she had been afraid of. There wasn't a single pair of underwear left. Now that she looked, there wasn't even another clean bra left in the drawer. Except... She pushed all the way to the back of the drawer and found the matching sexy pair that she had never worn.

Jenna placed the only clean panties and bra that she had access to on the bed and stared down at them blankly, contemplating her next move. Even in the dim glow of her cell phone light, she could see the intricate lace designs that had drawn her to them in the first place, the subtle floral pattern, woven with the dangerously sexy combination of red and black threads. She remembered both pieces fitting so well; but why hadn't she ever worn them before? She had bought them right before her senior prom, hoping to have that magical moment with her date when he would undress her and be wowed.

But that moment had passed. Her date ended up getting drunk at a party the night before prom and hooking up with some other girl on the couch right in front of her. It proved to be enough of a shock for her to just wear her plain old underwear that night and to make it a lot less intimate and comfortable than she had hoped. Now, the underwear had gone unworn, without a boyfriend or even casual hookups, or any other occasion.

It just so happened that they were the only thing she had. The more drawers she checked, the more she realized that she was out of everything that she could put on this late: pajamas, sweatpants, workout shorts. Jenna had put off doing laundry for longer than she had expected. Reluctantly, she slipped into the underwear, then the bra. The fabric felt welcoming against her cool skin, and fit nicely against her figure. There was no way she could go to sleep now; maybe, if she did her laundry at this hour she could have her privacy and wouldn't even have to wear dirty clothes while doing it...

It seemed like a pretty good plan. She checked the time, 1:12 A.M on a Sunday night. Jenna had never done laundry this late, but thought of the privacy, of slipping down to the laundry room in just her undergarments was too enticing to miss. Everyone was either studying or sleeping at this point anyway; there was little risk involved. She was still pleasantly buzzed from the party, and feeling confident.

With that realization, Jenna gathered up her strength and lifted her heavy hamper off of the ground. She hobbled over toward the door and just barely freed a hand to open it. The hallway light was stark, but there was no activity whatsoever on the floor. Excited, but still a little anxious, she pushed her way out and hurried to the stairwell. There was always time to turn back, and the hamper covered most of her front, providing a safe cover in case she should have any close encounters. But the stairs were empty too, and her journey to the laundry room proved to be as easy as she had hoped. No longer concerned, she pushed the door open to reveal an empty room.

Jenna was pleased with her good luck. She put her hamper down and began to pull her clothing out and into the washing machine farthest from the door, humming to herself as she did so. She had loaded all of her clothes into the washing machine and was searching around for her detergent when she heard voices outside. She froze. They were getting closer and closer, deep voices, male ones. She wasn't sure how many. Three maybe? Maybe they would pass the room without looking through the window or coming in. But she wasn't sure. Running out of time, she grabbed the hamper, pressed it to her exposed body, and waited for the moment of revelation.

Jenna had been right about one thing: the voices had been male. There were only two though. She thought for a moment that they were going to pass the laundry room, but instead, she watched as they turned to open the door and pushed in, each of them carrying full laundry bags.

"Woah... looks like we aren't partying alone tonight," said the taller of the two boys. He had black wavy hair and an otherwise light complexion. His features were softer than those of his blond friend, who was also staring at Jenna. She had never seen either of them before, but even in her embarrassment, she could admit to herself that they were attractive.

"Damn... are you waiting for your laundry naked?" the blond one asked. Jenna scowled, clutching her hamper tightly to her body. Her cheeks were warm, but chills were beginning to run through her.

"No... no, I'm not." She forced her frustrated embarrassment into a new direction, as she lowered the hamper to reveal her bra and underwear. If she kept herself hidden, cowering, she'd be ridiculed as a girl who made a mistake, forgot her clothes as if in a dream. She'd be vulnerable, open. But if she stood her ground, she'd convey that this was no mistake. She didn't care what anyone else thought.

"Oh... well my mistake," said the blond. His eyes were glued to her body, his lips curling into a smirk. The other boy let out a low whistle.

"Thought nobody would be down here, eh?" said the black-haired boy.

"I guess... but I don't care. I just wanted to wash all of my clothes," Jenna responded. "I hope you don't mind." She softened her voice, changed up the intonations. She was going for sultry now. She could tell that they had seen what she had to offer, and by the looks of their gazes, both of them liked it.

"Nah. Do you mind if we do some laundry with you?" the black-haired one asked. Before she could answer, he had already picked up his hamper and started across the room. The blond followed suit behind him, grinning dopily.

"Not at all," Jenna said. She looked back at her washing machine, full but not started. Then she remembered what she had been searching for when the boys came. "Actually, would one of you mind lending me some detergent?" she asked.

"That's not all I'd mind lending you," the blond one snickered. Jenna frowned, as the other boy tried not to laugh.

"I'm sorry about my friend. My name's Tomas. He's Jasper." He gestured to the blond one, who was still grinning wildly. "And as for the detergent, I have Mountain Fresh and he has Tropical Breeze."

Jenna half smiled at that. She had always been into blondes, but Tomas was even better looking up close. He had a perfectly sloped nose and brown eyes. His lips were thin and his mouth broad, to match his prominent jaw. He was thin, but from the looks of his arms, she could tell that he was fit. Jasper matched up to him pretty well, though. His lips were shapelier, and they curled nicely, automatically as if he were always smiling. His teeth were the straightest that she had ever seen, and his smile was overall one of the nicest. "Thanks... I'm Jenna. Either one's cool. I bet that mixed they'd be the coolest." She wondered if either of them had also noticed the innuendo beneath that.

"You can say that again," Jasper said. He pulled out his detergent and poured some into her machine, then dumped his entire bag carelessly into a nearby washing machine and repeated the process for himself. Tomas did the same, looking slightly amused as he poured Jenna some of his Mountain Fresh. With a satisfied smile, all three started their machines.

"Now what?" Tomas asked, directing his question smoothly at Jasper. "Should we get naked like her to make it fair?"

"Hey, I'm not all the way naked!" Jenna laughed.

"That way we couldn't tell on you, should any person of authority decide to join our little party," Jasper said with a wink. "You should be begging us to jump out of our pants!"

"Yeah, yeah..." Jenna rolled her eyes, but she couldn't help but smile. She could still feel their eyes on her. They were more discrete about it now, but she knew every bit of her that was covered in intimate apparel was being gazed upon. There was something extremely flattering about it, something empowering. She felt a surge of confidence, and leaned in to kiss Tomas on the lips.

Tomas hadn't been expecting Jenna to kiss him. He hadn't been expecting anything more than a thank you from the girl in the black and red lace bra and underwear. But here she was, her lips planted on his, her free hand touching Jasper's crotch. Jasper had nothing to do with his lips, and instead just stared at Jenna and Tomas, after letting out a heavy breath of surprise at Jenna's multitasking.

When she pulled away from her, he got a better look at her face than he had that night; the dark hair, the wide-set green eyes, the scattered freckles and the red ribbon of her lips curling into a smile. It was like a scene from a movie, the scene where a man has an encounter with a strange and mysterious girl in an unexpected location and time in his life. Only in those movies the girl usually has her eyes set on one boy. Tomas had noticed her eyeing the two of them, the way she pursed her lips as they shifted from his face to Jasper's. She probably didn't even fully realize it, but her body language made it clear: she wanted the both of them.

Jenna was smiling now, and reached a hand for Tomas again, this time grabbing his crotch confidently, her body close to his as she massaged him, up and down. Jasper was just watching now, looking half fascinated, half jealous as Tomas leaned in to kiss her again. He had hardly known her for ten minutes, but he wanted her to choose him. She must have already chosen Tomas; he was her one focus now. Her lips tasted like sugar and a hint of leftover alcohol, and it turned him on. The sound of the washing machines faded Jasper out of the picture, and the awkward stiffness that he had felt in the knowledge that his roommate was an onlooker had ebbed away.

And then just as quickly as Jenna's lips had found his, she had detached herself from him and was now on Jasper. It took Tomas a moment to realize what was going on, how it was Jasper's crotch that her hand was riding up so smoothly. But Tomas wasn't ready to give up. She'd be his way again probably, but he felt a primal urge to make sure it was sooner than later. He snuck up behind her and kissed her neck, then reached his hands around to feel for her breasts. They were soft, exposed and pressed up in her bra. The lace was a welcome pattern beneath his fingers, and he squeezed, hoping that the gesture of desire would pleasure her.

Jenna kept the focus on Jasper for a moment longer, her lips moving to graze his neck, then his collarbone. But Tomas persisted. He wanted her attention back on him, and that was what he would get. And he got it. Jenna released Jasper, and turned to Tomas with a smile, running her hand down his chest and under his shirt. He smiled with satisfaction and pressed his lips to hers, cupping her head in his hand. He could feel Jasper still there, placing his hands on Jenna's ass to maintain his place with her. Then Jasper wrapped his arms around her and pressed his body to her, humping her slowly.

Tomas had known Jasper for a little more than three months now. They were roommates and good friends, but not good enough that the presence of his body felt weird, or like any rules were being broken. Jasper wasn't touching him, he was touching Jenna, but Tomas could feel the slow pushing as his friend rubbed against her.

"How about," Jenna began. Her voice was breathy and sultry. "I take you up on your original offer, and you guys take your clothes off so I don't feel so exposed?" The real party was about to begin.

Jasper had never shared a girl before. He'd fought over one, yes, but never before had the battle for attention brought him so close to another male. He knew that this was the only way he would get her too; this girl had made up her mind. But who could resist sex in a laundry room with a hot girl, even if that meant that your roommate got to share a little? If anything, this was like the ultimate bonding experience.

He pulled off his shirt, his pants, and threw them into a vibrating washing machine. Now, like Jenna, he couldn't go back. Tomas was doing the same, but Jasper was ahead of the game now, and got to select his positioning first. He chose to be in front of her, but reached around for a handful of ass as he did so. Jenna exhaled deeply in his arms as Tomas came from behind and took off her bra. Jasper decided to work on a different area, and went down, down, until he was face to face with that sexy red and black lace underwear. He pulled it off and began to massage her pussy. It was already moist in his hand, as if he and Tomas were relieving months' worth of sexual tension. Her feisty behavior also proved to be in support of that, as she clawed hungrily at Tomas's face, scratching his back with her nails.

Jasper knew how girls liked it. He rubbed slowly at first, testing the wetness. Then he focused on her clit, rubbing faster and faster against it. She gasped, and Jasper felt pleasure in knowing that it was his work that caused it.

That's when he had an idea. He stood up, brushed Tomas away, and picked up Jenna and placed her on top of the washing machine. The smooth vibrations of the machine as it worked were sure to give her pleasure. Tomas hoisted himself on top of the washing machine next to hers, and got back to work on her breasts, treating them with his tongue. But Jenna was tired of letting them have all the fun. She grabbed Tomas's dick and started jerking him off, and then looked directly in Jasper's eyes.

"Fuck me," she breathed. Her confidence made his erection swell, and he didn't hesitate to pull his dick out of his underwear. He approached her and spread her legs, dick hard and heart beating with excitement. He wanted to lunge at her, but instead pressed slowly into her. It didn't take long before he picked up the pace and started fucking her; she was so wet that lubricant would have done nothing for them. She felt so warm and tight around his dick, as if she hadn't been fucked in a while. Jasper grunted and started fucking her harder, turned on by his discovery. She moaned and continued to jerk off Tomas, then bent her head over and started sucking his dick. Tomas was on his knees now on the dryer, and he sighed with pleasure, his body moving as he slowly fucked her mouth.

Jenna was unstoppable. The sounds of the blowjob and the sight of his dick sliding in and out of this foreign pussy sent chills through him, and forced him to stop himself from cumming just yet. Her breaths were becoming increasingly labored, her head bobbing faster and faster on Tomas's dick as she moaned. It was a rush to know Jasper was controlling those moans, or at least playing a large part in it. Tomas still had the breasts, and Jasper knew how women loved to have their breasts touched.

He started fucking her harder, harder, speeding up. She lost her grip on the blowjob for a second; her head was slowing as pleasure consumed her.

Tomas's dick barely muffled the sound of her moans. They were growing louder and louder, and Tomas fucked her mouth faster and faster to keep her quiet.

And then she came.

Jenna's whole body was convulsing with pleasure. She tried to scream, but the dick that was sliding in and out of her mouth kept her quiet. Both dicks were large enough to satisfy her, probably seven to eight inches each. It had thrilled her to see them pop out; she had chosen well. After months of sexual inactivity, this was a dream come true. Their attractive faces blurred together, and she could feel them watching her as she came, convulsing against the washing machine. Jasper's dick felt more prominent than ever now as she tightened against it. She felt so dirty, so in control; the thought of it made her writhe in pleasure, and reminded her to continue firmly bobbing her head along Tomas's dick.

She could tell by his face that he was enjoying the blowjob, and by the way he was fucking her mouth faster and faster. She almost gagged a few times, but she reminded herself to breathe through her nose, to leave her throat loose and open.

She closed her eyes, concentrating on not moving too much as her body screamed, yes, yes, yes!

That's when Jasper pulled out. She felt like he was still inside her for a moment, then all of a sudden she felt a hot wetness rain down over her chest. She felt the puddle grow, and drip over the side of her breast and onto the washing machine. Jenna moaned, aroused by the sensation, and by her pulsating vagina. Suddenly, that warmth spread to her mouth too, and Tomas moaned as he came. She could feel his dick strain against her as he released, and the cum pooled in her mouth. She swallowed as he pulled away, then lay down across the washing machines, her body still twitching in ecstasy.

The two boys were both breathing heavily, avoiding eye contact with each other, but watching her, the way they had this whole night. Jasper reached into his laundry bag, and pulled out a box of dryer sheets, offering her one to wipe off her chest and stomach. It was the closest thing they had to tissues in here. She watched as Tomas did the same, and offered her one of his, his lips curled into an attractive smile as he brought his box into the competition.

"April Showers or Fresh Breeze?" he asked.

2 D IS FOR DINNER

It was a little after eight when hunger pangs finally brought Rachel Johnson downstairs. She came with her hair in a messy bun, her blue eyes wild and wired after a day full of work, clutching her laptop with her rosy fingers. She was famished, moving straight for the kitchen where I was sitting at our table, my nose shoved into my book.

"Sup, roomie?" she said, tossing a wink my way.

We had been living together for two months now, long enough to have fallen already into this pattern. I'd spent all afternoon at the kitchen table, nibbling on carrots and reading, as was expected of literature majors.

I'd accidentally walked in on her once,

in an effort to hand her my utilities check, and there she was, her ass a gentle, pearly slope peaking over her mound of green sheets; her large breasts flattened against her bed.

She'd turned to look at me, confused at first by the intrusion, but then she had grinned, unmoving, and told me she liked to air out after she showered. I'd nodded and blushed, my eye caught on the protrusion of breast, the nipple barely hidden by the bed.

Since then, every time she shook them jokingly at me, laughing about how big and bothersome they were on her slight frame, I'd catch myself wondering what they looked like upright, completely uncovered without anything to weigh them down.

It would be such a change from how she was usually dressed, with short shorts covering most of her gorgeous ass, and the large, unrevealing T-shirt that she always wore around the house.

"I'm good, yourself?" I said warmly, moving some of my schoolwork aside to make room for her at the table. She planted her laptop down beside me, and gave me a grateful smile.

"Good! Hey Charlotte, you know how exciting it still is for me to have a kitchen this year and, well, would it be too cheesy of me to suggest that we have a cooking night tonight?" I knew, of course, that she was referring to the dorm rooms that we had been subjected to last year in our freshman year of college. The kitchen was Rachel's single favorite room in the house, even more so than her own room. It was a prime environment for doing communal activities, and one of the things that we both enjoyed was cooking.

I smiled at her. There was no way I could turn down that excited, puppy dog look. Besides, everything we came up with was always delicious. "Sure thing," I said casually. My heart skipped a beat as she grinned, then reached down to pull her shirt up and over her head, revealing the sports bra that kept her double Ds a secret, a secret that was bulging from within the bra, bursting to be free. I stared as she grabbed an apron with little cherries on it from the kitchen drawer, and tied it around her neck and then tighter around her waist, so that the outline of her breasts was clearly visible.

"You want one?" she asked me, gesturing toward the aprons. She had a few more of them, one with little roses and one that was a solid and sexy red. "I didn't wanna get my shirt dirty," she added, as if she had any reason to explain her change of attire to me.

"Yeah, yeah, no, me too," I said, distracted. The apron fit her body perfectly, curving to the shape of her ass, the angle of her breasts. "I'll take the red one."

She tossed the apron at me, and then began assembling some supplies: a set of measuring cups that she had gotten for her birthday, two bowls, a bag of flour, sugar. She continued until the table was lined with an assortment of cake baking goods.

"Red velvet. With cream cheese frosting," Rachel said with a provocative wink. She turned around and started to pour the dry ingredients into a bowl. I got the wet ones: the buttermilk, the eggs, and the food coloring that left the tips of my thumb and finger a bright red.

"Looks delicious," I said. She grabbed my bowl to combine our ingredients, while I stirred the batter into a perfect consistency. Rachel liked to dominate these sorts of activities.

"It looks better than delicious. God, I can't wait." She ran a finger along the inside of the bowl, dying it red with batter, and then pressed it against her lips and into her mouth, moaning in ecstasy. "God, that's good shit."

"Then why don't you have some more?"

I said, with a grin. I grabbed the whisk and flicked it playfully as if it were a wand, sending batter flying at Rachel's upper body. Most of the batter hit just above where her apron cut off; the perfect height for it to drip slowly down into her cleavage and for the more adventurous drops to trickle slowly over her large breast until it was stopped by her apron. She almost laughed, but stared instead, her mouth agape for a moment before she spoke forcefully.

"Clean it up." Her stare was just as forceful as her words. I surveyed the mess I'd made, her breasts heaving up and down in what was it, anger? I wasn't sure. I grabbed a towel.

"Sorry I—,"

"No, not like that. I'm not letting this batter go to waste. You made a mess. Now lick it off." She was smirking a little now, watching for my reaction. When I just nodded, she reached around to the back of her neck and untied the apron strings, then pulled it down to reveal her breasts bulging against her sports bra, her nipples visibly erect. "You've already behaved badly. Don't make me wait."

I started to give a spluttered reply, but suddenly stopped and moved towards her. I pressed my tongue hard against the lowest visible part of her breast, and then moved up, cleaning the batter from her skin and swallowing, pressing my teeth against her soft skin. I wasn't going to let her humiliate me. The batter truly was delicious, and it fueled my lapping. I grabbed her arm to steady myself as I buried my tongue into her cleavage, pushing my face down as far as it would go. Goosebumps sprang up on her arm, and she inhaled sharply. But there was no way I was stopping now. I tucked my hand underneath her bra and pushed up to cop a feel, and wiped the rest of the batter that had been buried too deeply into her cleavage away with my hand.

Rachel grabbed my wrist and pulled it up, placing my fingers in her mouth. Her breath was hot as she rubbed her wet tongue against them, and then tightened her lips to suck on them. She wasn't about to let me keep my dominance.

"Have you ever done anything with a girl before, Charlotte?" she cooed, shoving my hand back underneath her bra where she found it. My heart started pounding as I realized the exact implications of what we were doing.

"No," I breathed, my voice barely more than a whisper.

"Well, aren't we lucky that there's a first for everything?" Her eyes no longer resembled puppy dog eyes; there was a new fire to them, a confidence in her newly established power over me. "I promise I won't tell if you won't." Her voice was like a purr, reassuring.

Before I could respond, she yanked her sports bra off over her head to reveal two large, shiny white breasts, with soft pink nipples each the size of a half-dollar coin. She grabbed my hand in hers and pressed it back against her breast. "I said, I won't if you won't," she repeated.

"I... won't," I breathed, my heart pounding as she let go of my hand and reached, this time for me.

She slid her hand underneath my apron, up under my skirt, and ran it gently along my underwear. I let out a shaking breath and we both stumbled forward until she had me pinned against the counter. She wove her dye-stained fingers stealthily up into my underwear, so that her middle finger was rubbing up and down my wet pussy, taking care to roll back against my clit.

"Fuck," I moaned. I'd had my share of men do this to me before, but even the most experienced had never had what Rachel did: gentle, uncalloused fingers, and absolute familiarity with my anatomy.

"Having too much fun?" she teased. Her breath was a warm hiss in my ear. I shook my head. Her motions were perfectly timed, stimulating in perfect repetition. "Good. Let's stir things up a bit then." She reached onto the counter, and dipped her fingers into the bowl of unused red velvet batter, then gently moved her hand up my skirt again, her fingers sticky and cold. I could feel my legs beginning to give way as she rubbed it against my clit.

"God, fuck, what're you—"

"Easy, now." She helped me down, so that we were both on the kitchen floor, me leaning back, my legs spread weakly open. "Just let me handle this." Her voice was a reassuring purr again, and I nodded, submissively allowing her to take off my underwear. She encouraged me to lean back, as her head disappeared under my skirt, and then began to bob up and down as her warm tongue cleaned up the thick batter.

I gasped and reached down to grab a handful of her hair, lifting my skirt and apron up to watch her suck, then flick her tongue quickly against my clit as her fingers stroked my opening. In a haze of ecstasy and stimulation, I untied my apron, pulled my shirt off, and began massaging my own smaller, well-rounded breasts from underneath my bra. My eyelids began to flutter shut but I saw Rachel peek up at me, her lips curled into a pleased smirk. She stopped to unhook my bra and to strip off her shorts and my skirt, so that I was completely naked on the kitchen floor, and she was in just her underwear, a bright blue thong.

She applied some more cake batter to her fingers, and spread them along my nipples, making little circles with her fingertip, one nipple at a time. Then she began to lick it, sucking the sweetness off of each nipple, leaving a little red stain where the batter had been as evidence of our affair.

She slid her middle finger inside me, and I reached forward to grab her breasts in retaliation, playing with them, caressing them, pinching her nipple every so often to get a moan from her. Her finger was going in and out, in and out, so smoothly, so teasingly.

"Oh god, just fuck me," I moaned. It seemed to have been the cue she had been waiting for. She inserted her pointer finger, slowly, still teasing me, then began to move, faster and faster, sliding in and out of my slippery snatch. I tried to grip the tiles in pleasure, but it was beyond me.

"I'm going to make you cum," she breathed. "I'm going to be your first—the first girl to ever make you cum. Just don't worry about a thing, baby, I'm taking care of you." Her fingers were pressing deep into me, curving slightly, pushing against the wet, muscular walls of my vagina. "Just relax. You've been so good today, better than I knew you could be. What do you have to say for yourself?"

I gasped, moaning loudly. Her fingers went in and out, faster and faster. All I could think about were the spasms that were starting to shake my body, which were out of my control. "No, I can—oh my god, oh my god, oh my god!" The formation of sounds only added another thing that I was long past controlling. My legs started to jerk closed but she held them open, her mouth now descending upon my clit again, licking it with quick flicks of her smooth tongue.

"Say it. Say you'll be my good college dyke. Say you'll be a good girl." Her breath was hot and moist against my already wet pussy. "God, you're dripping. Don't you get any on the kitchen floor, now."

"I—I..." I let out a high-pitched gasp. I grabbed the back of Rachel's head and held it against my crotch, her words echoing in my head. I moaned loudly as my body convulsed in orgasmic pleasure, allowing the deep, stimulating sensation to roll through me, as if I had never been holding back. I could hear Rachel moan as

I did; her free hand had been stroking her own clit, and her face was twisted into a blissful grimace, her eyelids fluttering between my legs. Her fingers pressed into me, harder, and harder still, my vaginal walls tightened, contracting against them.

I had barely finished twitching when I tore myself away from her and crawled down to pull her hand away from her clitoris, so that I could have a go, fueled by the euphoric breathlessness that I felt rolling through me. I tested my own skills with the female anatomy, rubbing and prodding and licking to see if I, too, was as good as her. I wanted to be good for her, and her moans edged my drive.

I grabbed the whole bowl of batter off of the floor where one of us must have put it in our sexual frenzy, and poured some over the mouth of her pussy without the reserve that she'd had dabbing it on me. Rachel moaned softly, her eyebrows lifting as if she could hardly contain herself. I held her thighs down as I licked where I guessed her clit was through the batter with long, slow motions of my tongue, then whipped it faster and faster, her moans growing louder and louder, her chest rising and falling. It was almost like licking the inside of a bowl, but with the hot taste of sex and power.

Oh, her breasts. I reached up without moving my mouth, and pinched her nipple in between my sticky thumb and pointer finger. I felt talented, skilled; her gasps of pleasure made me feel powerful. It felt good seeing her how I had been: the naughty, vulnerable one, hardly able to keep from shrieking.

And then she came, with a low, wild moan. She took a few short, jerky breaths and shuddered, her muscles stiffening. That's when I fingered her with everything I had left in me. In and out. In and out. It went on until we collapsed together, a naked heap on the kitchen floor, where we remained for a minute.

"So... now what?" I asked her. The kitchen tile was cold against my cheek, and lying here naked felt strange; not unwelcome, but different. Rachel sat up, slipping on her sports bra again as I bid a silent farewell to her breasts that I was so in awe of. Her bright blue eyes would probably never look as filled with innocent excitement to me as they did earlier today. Instead they held a certain slyness, a sense of overt sexuality I had somehow overlooked, or that maybe she had hidden from me until this day.

"Now, we bake what's left of our cake."

3 MOBILE DICK

Laura had spent the last half an hour in her bathroom curling her hair. She didn't do it very often, but her best friend Sonia was throwing a graduation party. It was going to be red carpet themed, a chance for the girls to dress up in old prom dresses or whatever other nice dresses they had, or else come in something headline making and innovative. Laura wasn't the artsy type; she had opted to go with a red dress that she had found in her closet. It was a former Halloween costume, but it was pretty enough to make her enough of a belle, even if it was a little bit old fashioned, with its touch of beige and long sleeves.

She knew it was a good enough dress

for Sonia; a token of a good time they had together as best friends freshman year, which was when Sonia had picked this dress out for her how nicely it matched her tan skin and dark brown hair. Girls with darker complexions had to go for strong colors, like red, Sonia had told her confidently.

Laura checked her phone for the time, and cursed under her breath. It was 7:15 p.m., and the party started in only 45 minutes. Sonia had well-off parents who were funding the event, and had reserved a ballroom downtown for the night, to match the classy theme. The only problem was that Laura lived half an hour away from the area, and tonight her car was in the shop, where it had landed after an unfortunate run-in she'd had with a giant yellow Hummer.

Fiddling with her phone, she dialed up Sonia's number. The phone rang and rang, and went straight to voicemail. "Fuck," Laura muttered. Sonia had a strict policy of not answering calls while she was driving, which meant that she had probably left already, and was likely far enough away to not turn back and give Laura a ride. As the hostess, it was typical that Sonia would want to arrive a little early to make sure the drink table was set up, and that the actual red carpet that she had bought was being used properly, leading up to the stage perfectly in the center of the ballroom. Laura grabbed her phone and stuck it in her little black purse, irritated at the thought of having to catch the bus looking like this. She could hail a taxi, but they didn't drive by her street as often as was favorable and she was low on cash. She put on a dash of red lipstick to match her dress, and hurried out of her apartment.

Outside the wind was cool for spring, and the street smelled like fresh rain. She walked a block to the bus stop, enjoying the sound of her heels clicking against the pavement. She wondered what boys were going to be there, and how they would look dressed in suits. There was nobody who really struck her interest in her friends group, but maybe, just maybe she'd get lucky once she'd gotten her drink on.

Her phone rang, and Laura fumbled through her purse, grabbing it quickly and grinning when Sonia's name and picture flashed up on the screen. Perhaps she wouldn't have to take the bus after all.

"Sonia?" Laura said into her receiver.

"Yeah, where are you?" came Sonia's response. Her tone had the worried, vaguely irritated edge that it got when things didn't go as planned.

"Listen, I didn't remember that my car was in the shop until the last minute while I was getting ready, so I was going to ask you for a ride." She bit her lip. Sonia was a responsible person, who was often bothered by Laura's forgetfulness. She heard her sigh.

"Did you call me as soon as you remembered?" Sonia asked her.

"Well... I finished my hair first. I curled it just for the party," Laura said, hoping that her careful following of the elegant theme would appease Sonia a little bit. Still, all she got was another sigh.

"You could've brought your curling iron and done it in the bathroom here. You knew I was leaving early; you should've tried harder to catch me before I left."

"And carried a curling iron with me all night?" Laura asked.

"Look, Laura. The party's starting at 8 for a reason. It's a dinner party first, and a drinking party second. I don't want to make everyone else wait on you before starting. People are coming here hungry and I can't make everyone wait. Alice told me she hasn't eaten all day to save room for food and alcohol tonight. So you'd better find a way here on time or we're going to have to start without you," Sonia said.

Laura's heart sank. "Yeah, alright."

"I'm sorry. You just have to be more responsible sometimes, you know?" Sonia said. The comment stung but Laura just nodded.

"Yeah. I'll see you soon."

"Call me when you're here. Love you." Sonia's voice was softer, more sympathetic as she hung up, leaving Laura alone on the darkening, wet street.

Laura couldn't sit down at the bench at the bus stop; it had gotten all wet from today's rain, and Laura didn't want to ruin her dress or show up with any embarrassing stains. Instead she just stood by the street corner, holding onto the bus stop sign and twirling slowly around it on her toes. It was one way to pass the time, as she watched the cars zoom past.

A car or two honked at her, and she smiled slightly after realizing it was probably because she looked good. Still, her self-esteem was shot after her talk with Sonia, and a couple of approving honks didn't change that too much. She knew that Sonia just wanted to throw the perfect party, and this was her last chance to impress her Model UN friends, and she shouldn't take it personally that they wouldn't wait on her. She looked at her phone's time again and groaned. 7:25 p.m. A few minutes late would be alright, but at this rate the bus would probably take a good hour to get her there. Unfortunately she had no choice. She stood gazing out into traffic, reading the license plates of all them and counting which ones were from out of state. She got eight in five minutes.

Still, she was somehow the only person waiting on the bus here. She wondered if this stop could have been discontinued or if she just had really bad timing and had barely missed it.

That's when a maroon van pulled up to a stop just in front of her. It had white trim around the windows and a white stripe going down the side, and looked like it came straight out of the 90's. She watched curiously, as the door popped open and a brown-haired young man stuck his head out. He looked like he was in his early to mid twenties, possibly just out of college. When he saw her looking in his direction, he grinned, and threw his hand up in a wave.

"Hey, you! Come here!" he shouted. Laura looked around apprehensively. It was a busy street, and if anything happened to her she was sure somebody would take note. Besides, this man was too attractive to look even remotely creepy, and hearing what he had to say might be interesting. Before she could say anything he spoke again. "That's a nice dress! What's a pretty girl like you doing without a ride?"

"Oh, just waiting for the bus," Laura said with a little smile. She couldn't deny that she enjoyed the flattery.

"I see. Where're you headed?" asked the boy.

"Just downtown. My best friend is throwing a graduation party," she said.

"Nice, nice. Hey, where downtown is it? That's where we're headed," the boy said. Laura's heart jumped at the prospect of a ride.

"Uh... 3100 Monroe Street?" she said. "It's in a banquet hall right by the park."

"Shit, I know where that is!" another voice called from the van. Another boy popped out of the passenger door to the van and grinned at her. This one was slightly shorter than the brown haired guy, but still had a nice, masculine face, and was blonder. "You should ride with us! It isn't safe on the streets after dark, you know."

"Yeah, I guess not," Laura said with a little laugh. The second boy looked just as harmless, like a couple of frat guys driving around with nothing better to do. "If you guys don't mind. I'd pay you for gas but unfortunately I only have two dollars on me."

"Don't worry about it," said the first boy with darker hair. He smiled, and climbed out of the car to gesture her in. "There are better things than money in this world."

"I guess you're right about that," Laura said. Her initial instinct about the van was right; the inside looked straight out of the 90's too, with an old portable VCR player and a small old TV attached to the ceiling of the car. The middle row of seats had been removed, and there was a small rug where they used to be, separating the back seat where the boys must have been sitting from the font. It was an overall homey appearance; nothing too sketchy. She thought again about how Sophie would feel if she managed to not disappoint her and get there relatively on time. With a final glance at the empty bus stop, Laura hopped in and the van drove away.

"So what's your name?" asked one of the boys that she hadn't noticed upon coming in. He was a young man with black hair, sitting in the passenger seat, peering at her with his light eyes using the rearview mirror. There were four of them total, counting the driver, who she couldn't see beyond the dark eyes that glanced at her from the rearview mirror.

"Laura," she said, twirling her hair between her fingers. It wasn't a nervous gesture; she had decided she'd have to trust these boys until it was proved that she would have to do otherwise.

"Nice, nice," the boy who had first hollered at her chimed in. "I'm Chris," he said. And that's Damien, the other good looking one," he gestured toward the black-haired boy in the passenger seat.

"Fuck you, man. Don't forget about Jack and me," said blonder boy who had helped call her in. "I'm Evan. Jack's the driver."

"Nice to meet you guys," Laura said, offering a small smile. She recited the names in her head: Chris, Damien, Evan, Jack. They weren't too hard to remember when she put them in alphabetical order; Jack was the only one whose name jumped out of order, and he was sort of out of the way as the driver, anyway.

"Yeah, same," came a chorus of murmurs.

"So, you know why we offered to drive you, don't you, Laura?" Chris asked. He sort of stood out as a leader among the group. He had the strongest presence, and by the looks of the way his shirt fit, was the most muscular.

"Um, because you're going downtown

too?" Laura asked with a smile.

"Anything else you can think of?" Chris asked. His voice was smooth and deep, and had a sultry feel to it that made her blush.

"Uh, I don't know," she said with a small laugh.

"Well fuck, Laura," Evan chimed in. Chris shot him a look, and Evan just shrugged. "You're hot, what can I say?" Evan said.

"Oh, well thanks. I appreciate it," Laura said, pleased again by the flattery. "The party I'm going to is red carpet themed, so I had to dress up a little extra." Evan chuckled, but she wasn't sure at what.

"Cool, cool, sounds like a fun time. But hey, we'd like to ask you for a favor," Evan said. "Would you fuck my friend Chris for me?" He reached over and gave Chris a pat on the shoulder. Chris shoved him off with a smirk.

"Um... sorry? I mean, I guess," Laura said. She hardly knew how to respond to that, or if they were even serious. Chris gave Evan a look that was hard to read, but Laura could sort of make out him trying to conceal the same smirk from before.

"You don't have to listen to him," Chris said.

"Yeah, whatever, man. You see, he's just a really deserving guy, and he could use a little female loving if you know what I mean." Evan winked. "There's enough time between here and our destination, anyway."

"Wait, are you serious?" Laura asked. When there was no response her voice got smaller, more nervous. "Ha ha, good one. I'm just going to a party, I'm not a prostitute if that's what you think this is," Laura said softly. "I can promise you that not all hot girls are."

"See, that's where we disagree," Evan said. She could tell now that he was the most talkative of the group. "You see, hot girls are so used to having shit handed to them, dicks and all, whenever and however they want them. But when you reverse the roles a little, they get so good at giving back, if you know what I'm saying. You just have to open up your mind a little. I figure deep down in every hot girl is a hot slut waiting to awaken."

Laura shook her head. The little speech gave her chills, but it also stirred something inside of her. "You don't know me," she said flatly.

Evan shrugged. He was about to say something else when Chris jumped in again. "You don't have to listen to him," he said again with a laugh. "But then, it could be a fun way to pass the time. Or else we might just drop you off somewhere that you didn't intend for."

"You can just drop me off on the side of this road," Laura said. Her heart was starting to pound faster inside her chest. They had probably passed another bus stop that was more active than the first one by now.

"C'mon baby, don't do that," Damien chimed in from the front. "This is no strings attached shit, we promise we'll get you there on time. Can you be okay with that?"

"I don't know." Laura said uncomfortably.

"I think we'll be able to do a little bit of convincing," Chris said, as he leaned in toward her.

Laura could feel her breathing quicken. Chris slid his hand along her dress and grabbed her breast. Laura tried to jerk back, but bumped into Evan on her other side.

"Shhhhhhh... It's alright," Evan said, as if she was a trapped animal. He ran his hand along her shoulder, and down her arm, stroking it carefully. "We really don't want to do this by force. We aren't out to commit any crimes or nothing."

"Then don't," Laura retorted. She tried to jerk her arm away from Evan, but he held fast. Suddenly there was Chris's hand again, pushing against her breast. She gasped, but before she could say anything, he reached into his pocket and pulled out a blindfold. He tied it swiftly around her eyes, blocking out her vision.

"There we go," came Chris's voice. "Are you comfortable, baby?" Laura's heart was racing and she tried to pull her arms away from Evan again, but he held them firmly behind her back.

"I promise they won't do this the whole time," came Damien's voice. "This is just to help get you comfortable."

Laura was starting to panic now. She tried to kick, but Chris sat himself down on her legs, restraining the last weapon she had left.

"We promise we won't hurt you," he said. "You'll arrive safe and sound at your destination. You just gotta let loose, baby."

"Stop calling me that," Laura grunted. She put on her best straight face, trying not to show panic that she had misjudged these men.

"See what I mean?" Chris laughed and reached over to rub her breast. Laura could feel her heart racing as he tried to slip his hand down and into her dress, under her bra. His hand was cold and rough against her warm breast, and he squeezed it as if to assert ownership. Laura tried to move, but the attempt was futile. She could feel her nipple hardening against his finger, and her breath increasing with the action. But she said nothing that would give him the satisfaction.

Then she felt someone lift her dress and pull her underwear down. "Seriously, stop it!" she cried, and took another opportunity to kick, but Chris held her legs fast. She heard a clambering and a thump in the center of the van, and could only assume that Damien had gotten up out of the passenger seat and come to the back to join them. She felt the cool air from the van against her, and knew that she was exposed.

"Damn, that's nice," she heard Evan say. "What a sweet pussy you got there, hun."

"We have some things that we think will make you enjoy this," Damien's voice said smoothly. She felt a hand reach over and a finger run along the inside of her vagina. Laura shivered. She had stopped struggling in case they enjoyed watching her put up a fight, and her heart was beating faster than ever now at the touch, and the lack of knowledge as to who was doing it.

"This is the wettest pussy I've ever seen," Damien said. "Chris, man, she's lying if she says she doesn't want us. What do you say, Laura?"

"Fuck no," she muttered, trying not to struggle. His finger felt nice against her, but she wasn't ready to give up.

"I think we can convince her," Damien said again.

Laura heard the sound of rummaging, and then something cold and metallic was pressed against her clit. "Have at it, man."

Her breathing picked up with anticipation when suddenly the metal object began to vibrate at a frequency that she'd never been subjected to down there before. She gasped and moaned as someone started moving it, up and down against her clit.

"You like vibrators, Laura?" Chris's soft voice came. Laura whimpered, but didn't respond. Her fists were clenched, and it was harder than ever now to fight her arousal. She felt a finger spread her pussy, exposing more of her clit. Another hand had slipped underneath her dress again, and was massaging her breasts. "Are you going to try and tell us that you aren't enjoying yourself, you little slut?"

"Oh god," Laura moaned. Someone took the vibrator and began to push it into her vagina teasingly, then back to her clit.

"Turn it up," Evan said. Suddenly, the

vibration was stronger against her clit.

"Oh god," Laura cried again. She could feel herself on the verge of cumming with these strangers in their van. But she couldn't help herself.

"Tell us you like it," came Chris's smooth voice.

"I like it," Laura gasped. She arched her back, trying to fight off the arousal. But it was no use. She was going to cum and she knew it.

"Good girl," Damien said. The vibrator started moving up and down, up and down against her clit. Someone was sucking on one of her nipples now.

"Oh god," Laura moaned. It was the most intense arousal she had ever felt, as if this whole thing was a long setup to tease her into submission. "Just fuck me already. God, someone fuck me," she cried, struggling against her restrainers. It wasn't fair; going through all of this and not getting fucked at all so she could keep her pride intact was more torturous than just saying fuck it... literally.

"She asked for it," Evan said. Suddenly she felt a dick press into her. It was warm and hard against her skin, and slipped in with ease. She groaned loudly; it was thick and felt nice and big inside of her, satisfying her deepest cravings. But it was moving too slowly for the intense new feelings that were coursing through her.

"Fuck me faster!" she moaned. She wasn't being held down anymore. Instead of fucking her harder, she heard a grunt.

"Let me try." She wasn't sure which of the boys the voice had come from; for now her head was spinning, and her senses felt muddled and confused. The only thing that she was sure of was how aroused she was, and how it was inescapable. She wanted more. However, instead of fucking her harder, the boy pulled out. Somebody pushed her legs up, and suddenly the dick was back inside of her, fucking her harder this time. But this didn't feel like the same dick as before; it was faster, less thick, but just as pleasurable. They were taking turns fucking her.

Laura struggled to remove the blindfold, if only for a second so that she could see what was going on in the rest of the van. It was difficult with the movements of the van; the turns and lane switches were disorienting. Also, despite her initial reaction, she had never felt more turned on. She felt intoxicated by it; her movements were weak and jerky, and her limbs felt heavy.

"Ah, ah, ah!" she cried. She finally managed to tug the blindfold off, and saw that her dress had been removed somewhere in the process, leaving just her bra. It was Damien who was fucking her now. He smirked at her when he saw her looking and gave her a wink.

"Look who decided to join us," he teased. The other boys chuckled. Chris also had his pants off; his dick was shiny and erect, definitely the one that had been fucking her before. She felt her insides churn at his look of longing.

"Dude, this is so hot. She's so wet," Evan said. His pants weren't off, but his buckle was undone, hanging loose as if he were preparing for his turn.

"Oh God," Laura moaned. "I'm cumming!" Damien grabbed her knees and pushed them up high toward her head. She moaned even more loudly, closing her eyes gripping the seat for support. Suddenly, she felt something warm and hard push against her face. She opened her eyes to see Evan pushing his now exposed dick against her lips, trying to see if she'd take the bait. She hesitated for a moment.

"Are you gonna be the hottest slut we've ever had on board, or what?" Evan cooed. Laura whimpered and opened her mouth. She had never been so dirty, and just the thought of how bad she was being kept her going now. Evan's warm dick pushed into her mouth, and he began to fuck it gently, moaning softly. Damien was still doing his thing, fucking her until Chris grabbed his shoulder.

"My turn," he hissed at his friend. Damien brushed him away and pounded into her a few more times. When he pulled out, he came all over her exposed stomach.

"Careful, we can't get her bra dirty. She has somewhere to be," Chris said. Laura couldn't do anything but moan, as Evan's dick acted as the perfect gag, keeping her from speaking.

"Why's that thing still on anyway?" Damien said. Evan shrugged and reached over to clumsily remove Laura's bra, while she continued to suck his dick. She moaned as he grabbed her breasts and began to fondle them. Suddenly, someone grabbed her knees and pushed them up. Laura looked over to see Chris positioning himself, and inserting his thick dick into her again. She gripped the seat and closed her eyes.

Suddenly Evan started to fuck her mouth harder and harder, just as Chris was speeding up, fucking her faster and faster. Her mouth flooded with hot liquid, and she realized that Evan was coming inside of it. He moaned and pulled out, and she swallowed hard. Her whole body was turning warm, and she screamed, as Chris pounded into her a final time. She gasped and shivered; he was coming inside of her. She knew that it wasn't safe, but it felt so good. He pulled out for the final time at last, leaving her naked and gasping on the car seat.

"I hope you're on birth control," Chris grunted breathily. Laura was too exhausted to respond with more than a small nod. Damien had buttoned his pants up by now, and tossed her a towel, so that she could clean up her chest. He muttered something under his breath, but the only words that Laura made out were "hottest" and "slut". She feebly gathered her clothes and slipped each article on, first her underwear, then her bra. She pulled on her red dress last, trying to flatten it against her stomach.

"We're here," came Jack's voice from the driver's seat. Laura had almost forgotten about him, and felt a tang of regret that he hadn't gotten a chance to partake in the backseat activities. The van pulled to a stop outside of a beige building with a line of cars in front of it.

"See you later, sweet thing," Evan said with a wink as he pulled the van's door open.

"It was a good one," Damien said with a wink. Chris smirked as Laura just nodded and hopped out.

"See you guys, I guess," she said. She ran a hand quickly through her now messy hair, trying to make it look intentional. At least her curls hadn't all come undone; they were looser now, but still felt like they had some shape.

"Flag us down if you need a ride back," said Chris with a wink. With that he slammed the door shut, and the van drove off.

4 ROW MY BOAT

The windows were down and the music was blaring out the windows of Brett's car. The car was full, and any conversation that was made was thrown around by the wind. Josh could catch pieces of it every so often; simple words like "lake" and "shit dude" and "I think this is the right way" from where he sat in the back right-window seat. But the music won this war, and Josh had succumbed to it. He lay with his eyes closed and his head pressed against the window frame, listening as his short, dark hair was tousled by the wind.

"I think we made it!" Brett's shout was loud and audible as the music went into a lull. He turned the car toward an entryway with a big wooden sign that said "Lake

Wakulla" and the rest of the car cheered.

"You excited, Joshie?" asked Stephanie, the girl squished next to him in the middle seat.

"Fuck yeah," Josh said as he sat up, readjusting himself and preparing to get pumped. He and his group of friends had been talking about going to the lake for a long time, but today was the first time they'd actually come. The sun was shining and spring was nearing its end. The summer heat had settled in about a week ago, and everyone was excited to shake it off in the cool, clear lake water.

"I hear that the rowing team practices at this lake. Maybe we'll see them racing or something," Stephanie said, her eyes growing wide and dreamy at the prospect of hot boys.

"Yeah, I guess," Josh said with a shrug. He imagined them rowing; their large arm muscles straining against the paddles, glistening from sweat and whatever water splashed back at them. It was an image that stayed in his head until they parked and finally started to pile out of the car. Josh helped unload as Stephanie went to jabber with Allison about tanning on the beach, and the rest of the guys went on about the lake rentals.

"Dude, I hear you can rent a kayak for free if you're a student. Sounds awesome. Brett, I'll kayak race you," said Lucas, a tall, muscular young man with dark hair.

"Fine dude, but you won't beat me. I think everyone else should do it too. Josh, Lucas, what do you guys say? I know Steph and Allison won't," Brett said, rolling his eyes.

"I'm in," Josh said casually, an amused smile on his face. He knew Stephanie would retort with an angst-filled feminist response, and then tell Brett that she wasn't going to do it because he was an idiot. Her fiery red hair whipped around her expressively, and she turned as if on cue to glare at the lot of them.

"I'll race if I feel like it," she snapped, then turned to skip toward the lake.

"Yeah, sure," came Lucas's casual reply. His almond-colored skin was already glistening from the sunscreen that he had been applying to his large muscles while everyone else was unloading. Lucas worked out regularly, making him the most built out of the entire group. Josh sometimes caught himself staring at them in awe when Lucas was shirtless, but who could blame him? Suddenly, he felt Lucas's eyes on him. Josh could feel his heart pounding in his chest as he turned away and started walking.

"Guys, hurry up!" Allison called. Josh picked up the pace, heading in the direction of the lake with a cooler tucked underneath his right arm. Lucas's face was still fresh in his mind, but Josh hoped that he hadn't thought anything of the staring.

Allison gave him a smile when she saw him coming and stopped walking to wait for him. Out of all of the boys in the group, Allison preferred Josh. She would put her arm around him at parties, let her chin fall drunkenly onto his shoulder. Sometimes she would even give him sloppy kisses that he never reciprocated. He could feel her yearning pressing into him, but something about her just never seemed to spark anything inside of him. She never appeared hurt by his lack of response; she would simply get up and start again the next time they saw each other.

Josh didn't say much for the rest of the walk, but it wasn't long before the group made it to the lakeside. The girls began setting their towels down, as Lucas took out a football and tossed it to Brett. Josh placed the cooler on the hard sand, backed away, and signaled for the football. He caught it against his chest and threw it back at Brett, avoiding eye contact with Lucas.

"Oooh, look, it's the rowing team!"

Stephanie called from her towel. Her body was stretched out, with one leg propped up on her knee as if to call out to the rowboat, beckoning it toward her. "They're coming this way!"

"Nobody cares," Brett shouted, grunting as he tossed the football to Lucas. Stephanie rolled her eyes at him.

"Whatever. You're just jealous because you don't have their arm muscles," she said with a smirk. Josh looked off into the distance. It was true, they were coming closer. He could see their arms now, shining tan, some darker than others. Their shoulders were bobbing up and down as their heads adjusted to the force of the row.

"Ball!" The shout sounded like it came from Lucas, but Josh didn't react quickly enough to catch or even dodge the football. It hit him just above his collarbone, at the base of his neck.

"Fuck!" Josh yelled, putting his hand to the spot where the ball hit him. It was pounding now; it felt like he'd swallowed an apple whole. "God dammit, fuck."

"Whoa, sorry man," Brett called. "You took it like a champ, if that helps. It's what happens when you let chicks distract you."

"You alright?" Lucas asked.

"Hmph," Josh grunted, swallowing against the lump in his throat. Even the girls were looking back at him now, Allison blushing at the possibility that she could have been the one who distracted him.

But she wasn't. And neither was Stephanie. And he was grateful that at least nobody else had noticed for now.

One thing he did notice though, while everyone was looking back at him, was that the rowing team had finally pulled up on shore and was heading right for them.

The rowing team consisted of several men of different heights and skin tones, but what none of them lacked were muscles. Josh had been right in observing them from a distance. Their shoulders were the biggest he had ever seen; they were all grinning and giving each other high fives for their morning's worth of hard work and practice. There was one of them in particular who caught Josh's eye; he was one of the blond ones, with hair that was more golden than anything. It was combed back and wet looking, as if even the wind hadn't managed to dry it or lift it from its place.

The reason Josh had his eye on him was a mystery. He felt like he knew him from somewhere; that remarkably square jaw, his large grin full of white teeth, and his small, dark eyes that were shining in the light looked too familiar. But he still couldn't place it.

The rest of Josh's group wasn't looking at him anymore. They too had looked to observe the newcomers, the girls with their eyes full of hunger, and the boys with a quick glance and a shrug to suggest apathy. Surprisingly, it was Lucas who made the first move.

"Hola, amigos. Anyone want a beer?" he asked, opening up the cooler.

"Wow, free beer? Thanks, man," said one of the rowers.

"No problem. But if you wanna throw down for another run, we could have a full-blown lakeside party going in no time," Brett jumped in, seizing the opportunity for a party moment.

"Yeah, do it!" Stephanie cheered, raising her own untouched can. She had her eyes set on a darker-haired boy, and Josh could feel a strange sense of relief that it wasn't the golden blond. But where was he now?

"Dude, I saw that ball hit you from out on the lake. You alright?"

Josh turned around to face the voice and there was the blond kid, talking right to him. He cleared his throat, which wasn't pounding quite as hard now.

"Yeah man, thanks," he replied. His voice sounded croak-like. It irritated him to think that now of all times his voice sounded off. Josh had a deep voice that was usually very pleasant to listen to. "I'm Josh." Maybe if he learned of the other boy's name he would be able to place where he'd seen him before.

"Alex," he said with a grin. Still, it was nothing that indicated where he knew him from. Josh nodded and cleared his throat. But before he could speak, Alex spoke again. "Hey man, seriously though, that was kind of a hard hit. I'm planning on going to grad school for sports medicine, do you mind if we grab a beer or two and I take a look?"

"Oh... no, not at all," Josh croaked. He cursed his injury, but at the same time, it was working out pretty well for him.

"Great," Alex said. Everyone around them was chatting now, and a few boys were going to drive to the nearest gas station for some twelve packs. It was remarkable how well the rowers had integrated into the group. Even Brett, who had seemed the most apathetic, if not irked by their arrival, was chatting with one of them about football, and no longer seemed intimidated. He dipped into the cooler with ease, and tossed one of the beers to Josh. "Place that on your throat for now? It should help the throbbing. If you want to follow me we can take this somewhere more private."

"Alright," Josh said, placing the beer to his throat. The cold was almost jarring, but it was getting hotter out, and the chill that ran through him felt kind of good. The sensation was deeper than just the cold, though. He felt a sense of excitement as he followed Alex off into the woods without saying anything to anyone, wondering if maybe Alex was hiding something under his good intentions.

The strongest question that lingered wasn't where they were going, but it was whether or not Alex could possibly be gay. Josh hadn't come to terms with his own sexuality until recently. The thought of anyone finding out, his friends, his family, put him on edge. It had made him more cautious, more quiet and reserved. He had always considered himself a typical guy who chose not to act on an impulse that every guy had, until he realized that not every guy had such impulses. Still, he had never had sex with a guy, and only recently had he signed up for an online hookup site. Josh didn't want a boyfriend; he didn't think that he could handle one right now, without anybody else knowing or treating him differently. There would be time for that later in life. But a hookup...

it sounded enticing, just dirty and secretive enough for him.

But there was no way that a hookup is what Alex intended all the way out here. There was no way that luck could possibly be so in his favor. Still, they had been walking for ten minutes now, and had long been an ample distance away for a throat check-up. His throat had even stopped throbbing from the cool beer, which was now dripping condensation all over him.

"Here we are," Alex said, as he took a final sharp turn past some spanish oaks. Ahead was a small, secluded lake, only about twenty feet around. It didn't look deep either; maybe six feet at deepest. But the green color and beautiful clarity of the water was enough to take his breath away, if only for a moment.

"Wow, where did you find this?" Josh asked.

"I've been rowing here every year since I was a freshman; it's given me plenty of time to explore," Alex said with a shrug.

"But why did you take me here?" Josh asked. "Erm, I mean I like it, but why just the two of us, if you don't mind me asking?" He cleared his throat again. His voice had improved significantly from the last time he had spoken.

"I though it was a good enough distance away to give you time without talking much, for your throat to feel better on its own. With that whole crowd of people, you were bound to keep getting bothered, talking, and being miserable from the lack of improvement," Alex said confidently.

"Oh... wow," Josh said. He felt his stomach clench. Alex was probably just being a nice guy. He wasn't gay at all. "Thanks, man."

"Don't mention it," Alex said with a shrug. He opened his beer and took a swig. "Besides, you didn't look like you were having too much fun back there."

"I was fine. Just in pain is all," Josh said, a little bit bothered that Alex had noticed. The secret of his sexuality had certainly put a wedge between his relationships with his friends.

"Well alright. Either way, I thought I'd help relieve it," Alex said. "You wanna go for a dip? The water might also help your throat."

"Yeah, alright," Josh said. His throat hardly even hurt anymore, but swimming with Alex sounded like fun. Alex was in the water before Josh could even undress. He watched in awe as Alex effortlessly adapted to the cool water, and dipped under even where it was shallow. Josh pulled off his shirt, and began to wade in slowly. While his arms weren't as muscular as Alex's, he had the abs to make up for it. Rowing... swimming... That's when he remembered.

"Hey, I have seen you before," Josh shouted at Alex, who had already swum clear across the lake. "I've seen you online."

"Online, huh?" was Alex's response. His eyebrow was raised, and he was looking at Josh inquisitively. "I'm online. But where online?"

Josh remembered now. On the day that he had signed up for the gay hookup site, he had stumbled across a profile that looked like Alex. The name was different, but the abs and lower half of the face was the same. It was the smile and the body that he remembered; the rest of his face was cut out, probably for identity purposes. The interests Alex seemed to have matched up too, to the ones listed.

"That gay hookup website," he said. "Hungry4Adam.com." He hoped that he was right. Alex's name hadn't been on there, he could easily deny it, or worse, call Josh out on being gay if he wasn't.

"Bravo," Alex said. "You're the first one to find out about that. I used to have people coming up to me all the time and asking about the porn, but never that."

"What porn?" Josh asked. Alex gave him a look, as if annoyed with himself for assuming that Josh knew what he was talking about.

"I guess I can tell you, since I reckon you won't go spreading this around. I did guy-on-guy porn while I was at my other school. I really needed the money and no porn pays better for guys than gay porn. Of course, word got out, I got threats, lost some friends, and so naturally I transferred and decided not to join a frat this time around; frats have no secrets. Nobody here has found out yet. Except for you. Can I trust you to keep it a secret?"

Josh nodded. "So, are you gay, then?" he asked.

"I wouldn't say gay... I just like to have sex, and guys fuck harder than any girl I've ever known," Alex said. Josh nodded. It sort of made sense. "You look like you'd fuck pretty hard. That throat of yours sure can take a beating."

"You don't know the half of it," Josh muttered, before he could stop himself. It didn't mean anything; he had never sucked another guy's dick before. But right now he just wanted to seduce Alex into believing that he had, and that he'd be a good fuck, like he had said.

"It looks like there's a lot I don't know about you, huh?" Alex said. The water rippled as he advanced back toward Josh. It was a slight ripple, a testament to the smoothness with which he moved, as if he were gliding.

"I guess so." Josh followed suit and moved toward Alex. When they had reached one another again, Josh circled him slowly, as if he were a predator examining his prey. Alex just kept his dark eyes on him.

And then the lunge came. It was Alex who made the first move, lunging at Josh. He pressed his lips into him, kissing him wildly, latching on fiercely by gripping his shoulders. Josh might have fallen back had Alex not been so strong and steady. He kissed him back, his heart racing wildly as his tongue slid into Alex's mouth. This was his first encounter with a man, and a hot one at that. He gripped Alex's huge arms; the muscles were as hard as they looked. They were flexed; he was showing off now. He thought about Stephanie and Allison and everyone else back on the shore, and nearly laughed. But he kept on making out with Alex, as fiercely as ever. He slid his hand down into the water, where he grabbed his round butt; it was better than any girl's butt he had experienced.

"Now," Alex whispered. "Do you want to show me what that throat of yours is capable of?"

Josh didn't even respond. Instead he just went down on Alex, under the water to where his dick was. He had forgotten just how cool the water was, as it flowed through his short hair. But he didn't care. He pulled Alex's pants down and grabbed his dick, then began jerking it off. He found it incredibly easy, like getting himself off. He surfaced quickly, took a deep breath, and began to suck on his dick.

Alex moaned above water. His dick was hard, erect as ever, and he began to fuck Josh's face as he moved his lips up and down over it. Soon he knew that he would have to come up for air, but it didn't matter right now. He could feel Josh grabbing his naked butt with his hands, keeping his position as he went for the deep throat.

Alex gasped. The forest surrounding the lake was quiet, except for the sound of birds, and of the bubbles coming up as he fucked Josh. He moaned again and reached into the water to place his hand against the back of Josh's head as he fucked his mouth. The guy was good at giving head. Based on the performance, he couldn't tell whether he was a first timer or not. He let go of Josh so that he could surface for air, but it was another few seconds before he came up.

"Now I know about your breath-holding

skills," Alex said. "I want to fuck you so bad."

"Why don't you give it a try, then," Josh said. His heart was pounding. He wasn't sure he'd even enjoy bottoming, but it was worth a shot. Alex grabbed him and whipped him around with a smirk.

"Hold your breath," he whispered, then pulled Josh's pants down and pushed his head underwater, so that his back was arched. Then he positioned himself, and pressed inside him from behind. From underwater, Josh tried not to gasp, or do anything to make him lose his breath. He could feel water coming inside of him, with the dick, stretching him out. His face contorted in pain, and he wanted to come to the surface, to gasp for air. But he didn't let himself, until Alex had pressed his way into him deep enough to where he wouldn't slip out. "How'd you like that?" Alex asked as he pulled Josh's back up and out of the water.

"Ohhh," Josh responded with a groan. Alex smirked and began thrusting, in and out. He could tell now that Josh was a first-timer, and that was how he liked it. He positioned his hands carefully on his hips, moving slowly at first so that he could get used to it.

"Another thing about girls; they usually hate it when I fuck them from behind. They just want you in their vaginas. Guys, however... guys enjoy it. They love being taken," Alex said, smirking as Josh moaned again in response. He reached around and grabbed Josh's dick, and began jerking him off. "I've heard I'm not bad at this," he whispered.

Josh shook his head. It was beginning to feel good now, as he relaxed, especially with Alex touching his dick. He was right about being good at it; he touched it in the perfect spots, exactly where he liked it, as if somehow he knew. Josh knew he was going to cum soon from the combination of getting fucked, feeling so dirty, and being jerked off so well. Alex was pushing into him in a way that made him gasp with pleasure, pushing against his prostate.

Alex closed his eyes. This was it; he had found the perfect rhythm. He fucked Josh, faster and faster, grunting as he continued to jerk him off. The water acted as a natural lubricant, making the motions smooth and seemingly effortless.

Josh moaned. "Fuck, fuck," he cried.

"Come for me, faggot," Alex grunted. He could barely hold on for much longer. Josh was just so tight and took it so well, without falling forward or losing his balance.

"Ahh, God!" Josh yelled. He could feel it now. He was coming, filling the water with his semen as his dick pulsated in Alex's hand. That's when Alex came too. Josh could feel himself fill up with the warm, sticky solution. His eyes rolled back as it brushed against his insides, enhancing his orgasm. Alex pressed into him, again and again until he was completely done cumming, then pulled back, trying to catch his breath from the pleasure that had coursed through him. They rinsed themselves off in the water, each too breathless to say much.

"You want to do this again sometime?" Alex said after a moment. "I haven't really gotten to do any of this kind of stuff out here. And I imagine you aren't necessarily jumping to come out to those squares. Do you think we can keep each other's secret?"

"I think so," Josh said. His heart was racing. He was fascinated by himself, and by what he'd just done. Maybe someday he'd even be able to have a relationship with Alex that wasn't strictly sex. A forbidden romance of sorts. But he was thinking too much into the future. He pushed the thought away and extended his hand. "Fuck buddies?"

"Fuck buddies." Alex took his hand with a grin and shook it, then squeezed Josh's naked butt with the other hand. "What do you say we finish our beers and chill here for a little longer?"

Josh smiled. For the first time in a few months, he felt less alone. "I'd like that," he said, and opened the can with a pop.

5 UNLISTED

It was nine at night, and Marie was sitting on a park bench beneath the sycamore tree where she and Ron had first kissed. It was he who had asked her to meet him here this evening, bearing nothing but her pretty face. She had obliged, but brought with her a crumpled note that she kept balled up in her fist. She rolled it around her pocket while waiting for him, and every so often she would pluck it out and flatten it out against her leg just enough for it to be legible. The writing hadn't faded away despite the wrinkled lines that divided up the space where Marie had created a list of locations that ranged from "the beach" to "a garden" to "a walk-in closet."

Marie had started the list a few weeks

ago, around the time of her first month anniversary with Ron. She hadn't shown him yet, but since that time she had thought up new places to add to the list. Some of the places were ideas for romantic dates and locations for moonlit walks. All of the places were fun ideas of places where she could lose her virginity to him.

Marie still hadn't told Ron that she was a virgin. It was a topic that never seemed to come up in conversation, even when they mentioned their past relationships, or the few times when they had pleasured each other using their hands, or orally. Ron was a sexual man; Marie could often make out the longing in his gaze, and could tell by the firmness with which he grasped her from behind that he wanted her. But he had told her that he really liked her, that he wanted to take it slowly. That was after she told him that her last relationship from two years ago, while she was still in high school, had ended because of her boyfriend's uncomfortably fast pace with her more prude, sixteen year old self.

But Ron never questioned her further about it. He'd kissed her on the cheek and wrapped her in his arms, and that had been the end of it. She had hoped that this list she had made would show him that she wanted him, too.

"Hey there, stranger." Marie swung

around at the sound of the voice, a grin on her face and her grip tightening on the balled up note. There stood Ron, smiling down at her, with his dark hair neatly combed to the side. His face was smooth except for a little bit of stubble on his chin.

"Hey yourself," she said warmly, and got up to kiss him. "Shaved your beard, huh?"

"I thought I might as well look nice for our special night," he said with a wink, as he wrapped his arms around her. "Happy eight weeks, babe. I thought I'd take you out somewhere nice. After all, seven is my lucky number."

"Oh, you," Marie giggled. It was only now that she realized that it had been eight weeks; she preferred to count by months when things started to get serious, but she found his form of measurement endearing. "Where're we going?"

"It's a surprise, of course," Ron said with a grin. He was a tall young man, and incredibly fit with broad, muscular shoulders and a strong back. He was on the university swim team, and every so often Marie would watch him practice from the bleachers. Her favorite to watch was breast stroke; Ron always looked so powerful as his shining muscles dipped in and out of the water and his arms thrust him forward. His eyes were a brilliant blue, the color of the water that he spent so much time in, and his dark hair was wild and unkempt from constantly being under a swimming cap. She thought it was sexy the way he brushed it out of his masculine face, and the way he kissed her afterward.

"Off we go, then," Marie said cheerfully, and offered him her hand as they strolled off into the night.

Their first stop was a local oyster shack, rated the best in town. Ron flashed Marie a smile and whispered to her that oysters were an aphrodisiac. Marie rolled her eyes playfully, and clung tightly to his arm, beaming as they were seated and then served. Ron rubbed her leg with his hand from underneath the seat, inching his way from her knee to her thigh. Marie wasn't sure if it was the rubbing or whatever effect the oysters might have had, but she was getting turned on. She wanted to yank out her list and tell Ron everything, all about the sex she wanted to have with him and all the places that she had listed for them to explore. But she kept it classy for now, stealthily rubbing her leg up against his from underneath the table.

"You know... maybe we can go somewhere more private," Marie said softly to him, batting her eyelashes. Ron nodded in agreement.

"Yeah, not a bad idea. After all, the world is our oyster," he said, grinning at his own lame reference. "Come on, I have an idea."

Marie nodded and followed, her mind flashing over every wonderful memory they had made so far together. The dirtiest that she had ever felt with him was when they were in her dorm room together, while her roommate was sleeping. She had given Ron a blowjob just a bed away, hoping that her roommate wouldn't wake up. The secrecy and danger had given her such a passionate energy, that she could have had sex with him right there and then, but she had decided to wait. Just having him eat her out drew such animalistic, pleasured moans from Marie, that she couldn't even imagine keeping quiet for long enough to lose her virginity to him without waking her roommate up, let alone her whole floor.

They found themselves walking through downtown together, back toward the university where they both lived and studied. The lights were twinkling for them, around the shops and in the form of the full moon. The first university building that they came upon was the auditorium.

"I've heard rumors that the janitor never locks this building, because he likes to take willing students inside to have sex with him," Ron said with a grin. "I've also heard that once you're in, it's easy sneak up onto the roof. Want to test that?"

"Who wouldn't?" Marie went ahead and leapt up the stairs, then pulled on the door handle. The door was large and heavy, and it opened, slowly but surely. "I really don't want to run into a janitor with a student though."

"He's probably not that bad. He's supposedly in his twenties," Ron said with a laugh as they slipped into the building. It was dark, and the moonlight shining through the windows was their only light source. "I think I found the staircase." Ron pulled Marie to the left, and she felt the cold metal bar that would open the doors.

Together they went up several flights of stairs. Marie dipped her hand into her purse pocket, where she had last seen the note that she carried with her. She couldn't imagine a better place to read her plans to him than alone on a rooftop. She fiddled around for a moment, but felt nothing.

The note was gone.

By the time Marie had given up searching her purse, she and Ron had reached the roof. She mentally went over their trail, wondering where she could have lost it. Maybe she had missed her purse, and the note had fallen onto the restaurant floor instead. Maybe it had been knocked out as they were walking, or somewhere in the dark of the staircase. Wherever it was now though, there was no going back. And there was no way that she could figure out now how to present her plan to Ron.

"That was almost easier than I thought. Breathtaking view, isn't it?" Ron reached out to grab her hand, but both of Marie's hands were already occupied with the purse. "What're you looking for, babe?"

"Oh, nothing." Marie cursed herself in her head. The question had been the perfect opportunity for her to introduce her list, to try to remember what she had written on it. But she had wasted that chance too. She lowered her hand and grabbed his.

"Well, all right," Ron said. The view really was stunning. The auditorium building wasn't the tallest in school, but it was tall enough to still provide a wonderful view of the downtown lights and the expanse of trees around them, glowing blue in the moonlight.

"Actually," Marie started. "I had a list of places; a list of beautiful places, romantic places, risky places, sexy places. Places where I wanted to do things with you... to you. But it looks like I've lost it. I'd been meaning to share it with you." She held her breath, somewhat nervous as to whether or not he'd understood.

"Oh babe, there are a lot of places I'd like to fuck you too," Ron whispered with a chuckle, bringing his face close to her ear. Leave it to him to make his way through her ridiculous innuendos and tell it like it was. "In fact, why don't we share some right now."

Marie nodded, suddenly immensely relieved and turned on by the breath in her ear. "I remember I had written on there the beach... a lake... a closet. A bunch of public places. On an airplane, in a library..."

"How about at school? In a public building? Or maybe on top of one..." Ron's hands were resting on her hips now, slowly making their way along the line of her skirt.

"I was just about to add that," Marie said softly. She leaned in for a kiss, a passionate kiss with tongue and teeth. She bit gently down on his bottom lip. She wanted him to know that she was ready. That she'd been ready. She didn't even feel like a virgin anymore; her thoughts had been far too dirty for that.

"I guess we'd better start a new list... together. This'll be the first one we check off." Ron pulled her close to him, and resumed their passionate kissing. He reached over and slid his hand down her skirt, rubbing it against her underwear-covered pussy. His other hand was gripping one of her ass cheeks firmly, asserting ownership and desire.

Marie's hand slid downward too, and she rubbed his crotch aggressively, overwhelmed by her desire to fuck him. She was tired of waiting. She began to unbutton his pants while they continued to make out, and then slid her hands into his pants and grabbed his dick. It felt hard against her fingers, swollen with longing. He humped her palm slowly as she grabbed it, stroked it, eager to feel it inside of her for the first time.

Ron responded with matching aggression; he stopped kissing her only long enough to pull her skirt down, so he could slip his hand into her underwear. His fingers were cold, but her hot pussy warmed them as he rubbed against it, first feeling her wet insides, then rubbing against her clit in swift, even motions. Marie moaned and leaned into him. She was jerking him off now, and pushed his pants down until they had fallen past his hips.

"Here, babe," Marie murmured, and she paused her kissing him for long enough to gather her skirt and help him the rest of the way out of his pants. She threw them in a pile on the floor, and yanked his shirt off eagerly, running her hands along his smooth, muscular chest as she did so. She tossed it into their pile; a makeshift bed of sorts out of the only fabric they had.

"Good thinking." Ron pulled Marie's shirt off and threw it with the others, then lay her down on top of them. She hadn't seen him fully naked before; every time they had been intimate in the past had somehow only led to pants off, without the shirts being touched.

"I have a confession to make," Marie whispered with a coy smile. She kissed him before she spoke again. It was now or never. "I'm a virgin."

Marie's heart was racing, with sexual excitement, with anxiety in anticipating Ron's reaction to her declaration. In the moonlight, she couldn't see any shock, any rejection in his face. Instead he just smiled and kissed her.

"I know. It's alright." He pressed his lips to hers, biting her tongue slightly. He was all right with this talk, but he wasn't willing to stop. He was horny, and he wanted her.

"You do? But, how, who told you?" Marie asked, her heart racing again. Not many people knew, other than a handful of friends she'd known since high school.

"I just know. I could tell by the way you squirmed when I tried fingering you. Some other little things, maybe. But don't worry. I think it's cute." He ran his hand along her breast, so full and pale in the moonlight. Then he kissed her again.

She kissed him back, and pulled him down on her. "Well I don't want to be anymore. I'm tired of waiting. I want to fuck you right here, right now, unless you have any objections."

"None whatsoever," Ron said with a laugh. Suddenly his aggression heightened again, as if they hadn't slowed down for a second. He was kissing her all over, fondling her breasts and repositioning himself over her. Marie responded similarly, spreading her legs and wrapping them over him, kissing and biting his neck eagerly. Ron put the tip of his dick against her, and pressed slowly in. She could feel a sharp pain in the surrounding area, but the pain only aggravated her horniness.

"Ughh, just fuck me, babe," she moaned, as Ron pressed against her. He pushed harder and the pain increased. She yelped as he gave a final, affirming thrust, and he was in. It still hurt, but it wasn't unpleasant. She could feel him somewhere inside her, pressing against somewhere that nobody had ever gone before.

Ron felt the excitement within him as well. This pussy was his and only his for the spoiling, and it wanted him as badly as he wanted it. He began to thrust into her, harder and harder, as Marie moaned. The moonlight accentuated her beautiful pale skin and blonde hair. She was radiating; glowing with beauty and purity and youth. And he was the one who was fucking her, who had given her reason for these dirty intentions. A feeling of lust shot through him, and he grabbed her breasts, cupping them and feeling their softness in his hands.

With every thrust, Marie's moans were growing louder and louder. She watched him go in and out of her, watched as he fucked her. It was better than she imagined, better than the scenarios that she had been thinking up for weeks now. The pain hadn't subsided completely, but the surge of pleasure was enough to almost mask it. She thought of how sexy he was; how his muscles were pressing up against her, gleaming with a thin layer of sweat.

"God you're so hot," Ron muttered, thrusting up against her.

"Oh babe," Marie said, her voice a

whimper now. "Fuck me faster, babe. Show me what I've been missing. Show me what I can never hold out on again." Then she moaned, loud enough for her voice to ring through the night. Ron put a hand over her mouth, muffling her slightly, so her cries of pain and overwhelming pleasure wouldn't give them away. He was fucking her quickly now, his body close enough to her that her clit was being stimulated as well. She began to feel light and tingly, as chills ran through her body.

"Fuck, show me how much you like it," Ron hissed. Marie shrieked and he put his hand over her mouth again. Then her whole body began spasming and her toes curled as she came.

Marie was moaning, whimpering loudly as her whole body was filled with an ecstasy she had never before known. It was like how she had orgasmed when Ron had licked her clit for a minute straight, only stronger, and this time she was cumming on his dick, as it kept going in and out of her.

Ron groaned loudly. He could feel her body contracting on his dick, tightening repeatedly as he fucked her. He thrust into her one last time with unparalleled speed, and then pulled out and pressed his dick to her lips. Marie's eyes were closed, but she accepted it into her mouth without hesitation. He came as her warm tongue pressed against the bottom of his dick, and she waited for all of his cum to fill her mouth before swallowing.

"Fuck..." Ron murmured. Marie didn't say anything. Her eyes were closed as she enjoyed the remnants of the euphoric feeling. It almost felt like his dick was still inside of her, thrusting and thrusting. She could still feel the dull stinging sensation, but it was no match for her pleasure. Ron wrapped an arm around her, and lay next to her, naked on their pile of clothes. The breeze was just right, and the moon seemed brighter than ever.

"I can't wait to do that again," Marie said softly. Ron smiled and kissed her lips slowly, happily. She felt so safe in his big, muscular arms.

"Neither can I. I love you, Marie," he said softly. Marie's stomach was suddenly filled with butterflies and her body began to tingle, as if the orgasm had come back for a second run.

"I love you too, Ron." She wrapped her arms around him, and together they looked out at the night sky.

6 HALLOWEEN HICKIES

It was Halloween, and masks and colors were flying around the room. What had started out as a small gathering at Marsha's house had turned into a night full of festivities: a full-blown masquerade party with close friends, friends of friends, and even some strangers who had heard about it and were stopping by, dressed in costume.

Lydia was one of the initial invitees. Marsha was her best friend, and Lydia had promised her she'd be in attendance. She wore her black mask with a lacy black dress that she had bought her junior year, the one that pushed up her smooth breasts so nicely. It was jet black, the same color as her now straightened hair, which she had done for the occasion. She had invited her boyfriend Ben to come, but he'd told her he was going to be working tonight and that he'd see her tomorrow. She could still feel the disappointment creeping up inside her when she thought of how Ben rarely came to any of the same parties that she did. If he was ever free on weekends, he'd invite her to parties his friends were having, or punk shows that his best friend was playing in. But he wasn't into the themes Marsha would come up with, not even her best timepiece ones, like "Masquerade," "80s Prom," or "Roarin' 20s."

"Lydia!" Marsha screamed from the other side of the room. She ran up to her and pulled her into a tight hug.

"Hey, hun!" Lydia yelled back, reciprocating the hug. Marsha pulled back with a grin; her cheeks were flushed red with alcohol and excitement and her golden mask was lopsided.

"The party! It's such a success! My best one so far, I think!" Marsha squeaked happily. She pulled Lydia in toward her and gave her a big kiss on the cheek, leaving her eccentric purple lipstick mark.

"It could be!" Lydia said with a grin. She lifted a hand to her cheek when Marsha pointed at her and cackled.

"Got you! Can we reinstate the competition tonight? Please, please, please!" she begged. At the last party that

Lydia and Marsha had attended, Marsha had gotten drunk (much like tonight) and decided to have a competition: whoever could apply their lipstick and give the most cheek kisses to party members would be the victor. They kissed everyone at the party, boys and girls, on the cheek, leaving their red and purple kiss marks to be tallied by the end of the night. But by the end of the night, they were too wasted to even bother counting up the kisses.

"No way, I won last time!" Lydia said with a giggle. She gave Marsha a playful shove.

"No, no, no, no!" Marsha whined. She stumbled a little bit against Lydia and giggled shrilly, clearly the drunker of the two. "We didn't get to count for real!"

"Whatever, I know I won! I could feel it," Lydia said loudly. "I had two kisses on some people, one on each cheek!"

"Oh fuck off, that doesn't count!" Marsha said. "C'mon, Lyd, it'll be fun! This party will never be as good as my other ones if I'm not running drunkenly around with my best friend in the whole world the whole time. Seriously, don't leave my sight and stop being bummed about Ben."

"Shut up, I'm not thinking about it!" Lydia retorted with a little frown. "I mean, I guess a little, but..."

"Then just drink more! Here, you can have my drink!" she said, handing over the metal water bottle that she had been carrying around. Marsha carried that thing everywhere and at parties always filled it with alcohol. She said that the red solo cups were trashy, and she liked to be more discrete. Also, she got to keep the leftover alcohol for later.

"It's okay, I can get my own," Lydia protested.

"Yeah, but you won't," Marsha said. "Which is why you're keeping mine. I shouldn't drink more anyway," she said with a giggle. "Seriously! Drink it or you'll hurt my feelings."

"Fine," Lydia said, rolling her eyes. She chugged a bit and winced—Marsha made her drinks stronger than anyone, man or woman, she had ever met. Whenever she teased Marsha about it, Marsha would wink and tell her that it wasn't called alcoholism until after you had graduated from college.

"Ew, don't make that face! That's your ugly face!" Marsha teased. "Now come on, let's play!"

After another few minutes of drinking Marsha's devilish concoction, Lydia's throat was burning enough that she felt ready to play. She pulled out her pocket mirror and re-applied a fresh layer of her deep red lipstick.

"God you look hot. Now let's go!" Marsha said excitedly.

"Alright, give me a minute." Lydia tucked her lipstick and mirror back into her purse, and then stared off into the crowd, as if contemplating. Then she turned around and kissed Marsha quickly on the cheek. "Gotcha, bitch!"

"Fuck you!" Marsha yelled, and ran off into the crowd. Lydia took another swig of the drink and followed suit, running in the opposite direction, her lips ready.

"Hey, you!" Lydia called to a kid she knew from her freshman and sophomore dorms, whose name she usually forgot at parties. The boy turned to her confused, and she grabbed his face, and pressed her lips to his cheek.

"Just playing a game with my friend," she shouted at him once she pulled away. "I hope you don't mind." The boy still looked bewildered, so Lydia just gave him a wink and walked away. If she was lucky, most of these people were too drunk to recognize her with her straightened hair and black mask.

She was glad that Ben wasn't there for this. When Ben wasn't at the parties, Lydia usually behaved herself, with one exception. It was a night a few months ago, and she got so drunk she ended up making out with one of Marsha's roommates, Sandy. But Lydia wasn't a cheater; she thought girls were attractive, but at the end of the day, all she wanted was a nice dick. Besides, she had been under the influence of alcohol. Still, she had never told Ben about the incident, just in case.

She continued the game for the next half hour, intermittently chatting with whomever she ran into and sipping on more of the drink Marsha had given her. She was significantly wobblier by the time she planted her fifteenth kiss. For this one, Lydia grabbed the cheeks of one of her girlfriends and pulled her toward her. She drunkenly missed, leaving a lipstick mark on the corner of the girl's mouth.

"Sorry!" she squealed, then giggled and walked away, back into the crowd. It's still counted, even if she had missed her mark a little bit.

She was looking down at her drink when she felt her shoulder slam into something hard. Stunned, she nearly dropped Marsha's cup, and fell back a little bit from the force of the collision.

"My bad," came the deep voice of the man that she had bumped into. He was tall with dirty blond hair that fell around his maroon mask; nobody Lydia recognized. The mask was made of some sort of fabric that looked as soft as the hazel eyes that stared back at her through the holes. Lydia laughed slightly and shook her head.

"No, no, that was all my fault. I'm sorry," Lydia said.

"Don't worry about it," he said with a smile. He moved to walk away when Lydia called to him again.

"Hey! What's your name?" she asked. The man turned back, the smile still on his lips, but more devilish this time.

"Why should I tell you that? That would ruin the fun of the masquerade theme, now wouldn't it?" he asked.

"Would it?" Lydia slurred. The man just shrugged.

"Maybe not. But I'm still not sure if you've earned it."

"Oh, really?" Lydia said with a smirk. She could feel a new game coming on, and the prospect excited her. "Well then, tell me how I would earn such a thing." Her voice transformed into a British accent as she spoke.

"I dunno. For starters, I've noticed you've been kissing half the party, but you haven't offered to kiss me yet." There was a twinkle in his eyes, an enchanting look that threatened to pull her in.

"Oh, I guess I forgot," Lydia said with a small laugh. "Do you want one?"

"Absolutely," he said. She nodded, and leaned into him, her heart racing. This kiss wasn't any different from any of the others; she didn't know why this one made her nervous, why it made her so desperately try not to think of Ben as her lips kissed his stubbly cheek. The stubble was a lot like Ben's, but less coarse somehow. She kissed the boy hard, so that lipstick mark would stick. But when she pulled back, the mark was so faint she could hardly see it.

"Hold on," she said with a frown. She reached into her small black purse and pulled out her tube of lipstick, which she slowly applied to her large, smooth lips, using her cell phone as a mirror. When she was done, she put her supplies away with a coy smile. "Hope you don't mind."

"Not at all," said the masked man. "Plant one on me." Lydia laughed and then puckered up and leaned in to kiss him again. She pressed her lips into his soft, prickly cheek, lingering for a moment. His cologne smelled like fresh pine needles, and for a moment, she could have sworn she felt his cheek lift into a smile. She pulled away and admired her work: it was the finest kiss mark yet, perfectly shaped and colored.

"Perfect," Lydia said with a laugh.

"Thanks." She teetered a little bit, and then steadied herself, unsure of whether she should walk away.

"Don't mention it. You just want one?" His eyes were sucking her in again, twinkling with something that she suddenly recognized as desire. She felt a rush of excitement, but then she thought of Ben and felt the horrible plummet of guilt.

"Yeah, unfortunately it's only the one that counts," she said with a laugh. Why did she say that it was unfortunate? She thought of Ben and cursed herself in her head. "I... I'm playing a game with my friend."

"We'll make it count," he said. Before Lydia could react, he leaned in and kissed her on the lips. Lydia froze, her heart pounding. She was too shocked to react; her limbs were stiff as images of Ben flashed before her eyes. But those images were blurred from the haze of the alcohol, and combined with images of Ben reluctant to come to the party, his apathy toward her friends. There was no way Ben would see this; most of the people here didn't know who she was anyway, given the anonymity that masks provided. It was sort of liberating and provided her with a rush of energy. The man pulled her close, so that her breasts were pushed up against him.

Slowly, she started to kiss him back, letting the alcohol take her away to be enthralled by this mysterious stranger. His tongue flicked against her teeth, urging her to let him in.

"Do you wanna go somewhere more private?" Lydia whispered.

"Follow me," the man said with a wink. He grabbed her hand and pulled her through the crowd. Her stomach churned uncomfortably at the intimacy of his touch, and she pulled her hand away. He turned to look at her to see if she was still following him. Lydia looked around. The party was going on as normal, without anyone paying attention to them, or at least not that she could make out. Her head was spinning and the colors were blurred. The man came back and grabbed her hand, tugging her with him again. He pulled her into a dark room, just barely illuminated by the moonlight streaming in through the curtains. The shadows were blue and eerie, but they enhanced the man's features: his masculine jaw, and his sparkling eyes. He shut the door, but the sound of the party was still loud and clear behind closed doors.

"I don't know about this," Lydia whispered. Sobriety still hadn't kicked in, but sense had paralyzed her.

"What's the problem? You don't want this?" He started unbuttoning his shirt slowly to reveal a strong, muscular chest with great definition, and the perfect wave of chest hair.

Lydia shuddered. "It's not that. It's just—"

He silenced her by pressing his lips to hers again, pulling her in once more.

Lydia melted into him as he reached under her dress and touched the inside of her thighs. She kissed him back and ran her hands up under his shirt, against his exposed chest. He grabbed her aggressively, picking her up and pushing her against the bed. She kissed him sloppily back. She felt so dirty, so irresponsible. It was too much at this point for her mind to move past her desire. She wrapped her legs around him and started getting aggressive, kissing his neck and chest, biting his skin. Suddenly, the door swung open, and two people stumbled in, wrapped up in each other's embrace, kissing each other fiercely. The man was masked, but Lydia recognized him as one of the boys whose cheek she had kissed at the party. It was one of the first ones, a dark-haired man with a neatly tamed beard and a strong brow. The girl's mask was off; she wore it pushed up on her forehead, so that it bunched up her messy hair in the back. Lydia gasped when she saw her face.

The girl was Marsha's roommate, Sandy, the one who Lydia had made out with at one of the parties. She was also the girl who lived in this room.

"What're you doing in my bed?" Sandy blurted. She had pulled away from the dark-haired boy and was swaying, staring through the dark. Lydia pushed her masked man off of her and clambered to her feet, trying to quickly straighten her dress out. Her heart was pounding. Sandy knew about Ben. Why had she been so stupid as to follow this man here? Maybe there was still time for her to run out of the room before her identity was potentially compromised. Suddenly, Lydia had an idea. She reached for her man and snatched his maroon mask, then stuffed her own mask into her bra. Sandy had complimented her mask earlier on in the night; maybe, just maybe with a different one she'd be too drunk to realize she was looking at the same girl.

The lights flickered on just as she was pulling the mask over her eyes. Lydia blinked, trying to adjust to the light. She heard a gasp, and winced, preparing for Sandy's exclamation of shock.

"Aaron?" Sandy said. "What's going on?" Lydia turned to see Sandy staring right at the man whose mask she had stolen, the man who she had begun to cheat on Ben with. His eyebrows were much darker than his hair, and he was staring at Sandy with his eyes wide, like a deer caught in headlights. His shirt was still unbuttoned, his chest exposed.

So Aaron was his name. And Sandy knew him.

"Not much. Sorry, is this your room?" he asked Sandy.

"You betcha," she said with a wink. Sandy started to advance toward him, in a manner that exerted sexuality. She was obviously interested in him. "And who's this?" she slurred, pointing to Lydia. Lydia could feel her chest swelling with relief. Sandy didn't know who she was. She was safe for now. "She's cute. Were you going to fuck?"

"Who knows?" Aaron said with a wink. "Who's your partner?"

"Josh," came the gruff voice of the bearded man.

"We were going to fuck," Sandy said. "So you're gonna have to get out. Unless you wanna share the room."

Lydia felt her heart skip a beat. She didn't dare speak for fear of Sandy recognizing her voice. All she could do was look to Aaron and await his response.

"We'd love to," came his sly reply. In an instant, the lights were off again. She heard Sandy giggle and run across the room. There was the sound of kissing, and Sandy was on Josh again, just like she had been when she first came into the room. Lydia felt a hand brush against her breast and realized that Aaron had come for her in the dark.

Aaron pulled her close to him, reaching around to grab her ass from under her dress. He slipped his hand up higher, then back toward the front of the dress. He grabbed her underwear and tugged it down, then fell to his knees and put his head under her dress. Lisa gasped; she felt her knees weaken as his tongue flickered against her. He pulled her legs apart just a little, enough to give him room to expose her clit, and then begin licking it. She could hear Sandy moaning in the background, and a couple of grunts coming from Josh. A moan escaped Lydia's lips, too, despite her attempt to keep from making any sounds that could identify her. The sounds and smells of arousal were heavy in the room, and they were making her almost as horny as Aaron's tongue. She crouched down, and then fell to the floor, unable to hold her stance any longer.

"Oh God," she whispered. It was better than what Ben did to her, more full of lust and skill. Aaron's head popped back up and he kissed her on the lips. She kissed him back passionately, unable to resist him any longer. He pulled her dress over her head, throwing that and the black mask that was inside of it to the floor. Lydia reached over to help him, taking off her own bra. Aaron's white teeth glistened as he grinned in the moonlight. He took off his pants, leaving them on the floor.

"Fuck me," she heard Sandy hiss across the room. Lydia closed her eyes and groaned. Aaron's underwear was off now, too, and he put his dick up against her face. She gasped when she held it. It was a good inch or two larger than Ben's. She felt dirtier than she had in her life, and the fact that she might get away with it thanks to the mask fueled her passion. She put the dick in her mouth and started sucking it. Aaron groaned, and started humping her face slowly, helping her out with her back and forth motions.

"You're so good," he whispered. "Are you going to tell me your name?" He pulled his dick back, and repositioned himself on top of her. The sounds from Sandy and Josh were growing louder; they could hear the slap of her getting fucked.

"Shhhh," Lydia whispered. She grinned. "This is all part of the fun." Aaron smiled.

He leaned in and lifted up her knees.

"You ready to get fucked?" he whispered as he massaged her exposed breasts, rolling his thumbs around her nipples.

"Oh fuck, you know I am," she whispered. He lifted her legs higher and slid his dick into her, slowly at first while Lydia moaned. It was wet enough for him to start moving faster and faster. She gasped; she had never had anyone fuck her like this before, getting started so quickly. She could feel his chest rubbing against her, the friction of their fucking stimulating her clit. She moaned and dug her nails into his shoulder, overwhelmed by the sensation.

"Fuck, it's too good," she whimpered. Aaron smirked and began to fuck her faster.

"Are you gonna cum for me?" he hissed. When she didn't answer, he spoke again. "You're a dirty one, and dirty ones always do."

"You don't know me," Lydia managed to whisper in between gasping breaths. She knew she was going to cum though, she couldn't deny it. She was going to cum faster and harder than ever before. She could already feel it quaking through her body, feel herself letting loose as Sandy's sexual shrieks filled the bedroom.

"Oh, but I do know girls like you. Won't even take off your mask," Aaron said with another smirk. Lydia gasped. She could feel herself starting to cum, her body starting to get warm and lightheaded, as if she had just passed some threshold.

"Fuck me. Fuck me harder," she moaned as she began to cum on his dick. She gasped and squirmed, wrapping her legs around him higher and more tightly than ever before. She placed her own palm over her mouth, trying to keep her screams from overpowering Sandy's to the point of recognition. Aaron took the hint and held her legs in position, then began to thrust harder and faster than ever before as Lydia continued to muffle her screams. The slaps of him slamming into her rang through the room as Josh slammed into Sandy, and only furthered her arousal.

Lydia could feel her body weaken, her toes were curling, and she was going limp again.

"Cum for me, please," she begged, in a voice that was a little louder than a whisper.

"You fucking know," was all that Aaron managed to say. He slammed into her, again and again, and then turned up his speed another notch. He grunted, gasping for air.

"You guys are so hot!" came Sandy's drunken voice. "That was the hottest sex ever!"

"Oh fuck," Aaron groaned. At the last minute, he pulled out and shoved his dick against Lydia's mouth. Lydia moaned and put her mouth around his dick, as he pulsated and came in her mouth. She moaned and swallowed, gasping for air when she was done. She lay there, limp and naked, her mask sweaty and crooked on her face. She readjusted it and slowly sat up, pulling her hair back into a bun.

Aaron stayed on the floor, not moving except to put on his underwear.

"Will I ever know your name?" he whispered. Lydia felt her chest tighten. She especially couldn't say anything now.

"Not tonight," she said.

"Maybe some other time then," said Aaron. "You can keep the mask. It looks better on you anyway."

"Maybe. Thank you. Unfortunately, I have a game to get back to," Lydia said. She wondered if Marsha had spent the night looking for her, and just barely remembered to grab the bottle that she had put down.

"Sorry to see you go. Good luck," Aaron said. Lydia pulled her final article of clothing back on and stumbled to her feet. With that, she opened the door and slipped out of the room, forgetting her own mask on the floor, where it had fallen out of her dress.

7 BODY ROCKING TONIGHT

The entire club was pulsating, dancing with Jackie as she shook to the music, her body flexing, hips gyrating. Lights were darting across the crowded dance floor, shimmering, the bright beams casting shapes of every color: green, pink, yellow, and purple. The beams drifted across the floor and cut through the clouds of smoke from cigarettes and weed that the occasional partier managed to sneak inside.

Here, Jackie felt like a bird dancing above a city on fire, lights flashing desperately around her, surrounded by a blast of Drake, then Jay-Z. She was a little too drunk for a college freshman and a little too underage for her occasional wobble as she danced. She was tall in her heels, prancing around with the music about an inch above every other girl, a healthy 5'9" with them on.

Her girlfriends dancing beside her had all found male partners that were grinding up against them, and she was no exception. A tall dark male had his body pressed to hers, his breath heaving against her neck as he thrust with the music, pushing up against her to the loud beat of the bass. She had been coy at first; she'd avoided his eyes and cautiously moved away from him when he told her that his name was Andre. But after offering her a few drinks, which her friends had encouraged her to take, he had gotten her right where he wanted her, smiling softly against him, her eyes closed and her brow furrowed in smooth concentration as she tried to keep moving to the right beat, to keep rhythm with him.

If Jackie were a bird dancing above a fiery city, Andre was the handsome male bird equivalent, doing a mating dance around her, ignoring the flames and the rest of the world, just reveling in the music and the lights with her. She had tried to talk with him, to shout over the music where she was from, what year she was in, but the effort proved futile. In the end, she had decided to just give in to her more primal desires and dance with him. It wasn't too big of a step, she thought. It wasn't even as big of a step as talking to him would have been, really. She had been nervous about meeting boys, especially at a club. Her older sister had been sure to warn her of the predator-type, who would go around fingering every girl they could on the dance floor until they could get one to sleep with them. Something about dancing in Andre's arms though, which had felt sweaty and foreign at first, now after a few drinks and an hour of dancing, felt safe.

The music shifted, and one of her girlfriends, Penny, tapped her on her shoulder. Her blonde hair was tied up in a messy bun, and she fanned the frame of sweat around her face with a quick motion of her tan hand. Her small pink lips were mouthing the words, 'LET'S GO,' as she tried to catch her breath from overexertion. Jackie stared blankly at her for a moment, and then reached into her bra to pull out her phone, where she had stashed it for safekeeping. The time read 1:30 a.m.; the club was going to close in 30 minutes anyway, and the crowd had hardly thinned. She nodded slightly at Penny, and then started to pull back away from Andre, who was still breathing into the nape of her neck, just below where her black hair met her skin. He didn't let go of her hips as she pulled back, but instead he loosened his grip so that she could turn around to face him.

"I have to go," she shouted. Andre shook his head, studying her, and leaned his ear close to her. The blasting music was relentless. Jackie repeated herself, her lips pressed to his ear. "My friends are leaving, I have to go. I'll see you around though." She had enjoyed dancing with him; he had a very suave way about it, and was almost perfect with the timing of his rhythmic thrusts.

"You sure you can't stay a while?" Andre pressed his lips into her ear so that she could hear his response, nibbling a little bit on the edges. "I'll buy you another drink. Hell, I'll even take you back home when we're done."

The sensation sent a chill through her spine, and she stepped back, smiling slightly, unsure of how to respond. She turned to her girls, and repeated his proposal as a shout in Penny's ear. Penny eyed Andre, her eyes wide and excited, and pulled Jackie in close to her.

"He's cute, why don't you go for it, and call us if there's any trouble? We'll come pick you up if you're uncomfortable, promise." Her patterns of breath matched her excitement that was in her eyes, and her upbeat enthusiasm. Jackie shrugged, and nodded, the excitement transferring to her all of a sudden.

"Okay, if you think so." She waved

goodbye to Penny and the rest of her girlfriends, who watched her on their way out, waving each time she caught their eye. Their white skin was practically glowing as the lights danced and the crowd consumed them, except for the tanner Penny.

Jackie turned back to Andre, who was grinning at her now.

"Good choice. Stay here, I'll get us some more drinks." With that, he pushed his way through the crowd over to the bar, where he flashed his wallet at the bartender. Jackie watched his slick motions, the presence that he commanded while standing there at the bar. He had chosen an ideal spot, and didn't have to wait more than a minute before the bartender came to take care of him, while other drunken clubbers waved empty cups. Jackie turned to sway distractedly to the music, no longer watching Andre, when a body pushed up against her from behind.

"Glad your b-oh." Jackie looked in surprise to see that another boy had taken Andre's place behind her, a blond one, whose flat body was now pressed against hers, with his wide hands sliding down her thighs. She kept dancing, her intoxication ebbing off enough for her to be slightly bothered by the newcomer that she would have to become accustomed to. She squirmed uncomfortably as the new boy rubbed her right thigh, his hand inching closer and closer to her pubic area. She started to pull away, but the boy held tight.

And just like that, his hand was gone. Andre was back and the blond had shrunk back into the crowd after a barking exchange that she had barely been able to follow. He wrapped a strong arm around her and offered her a drink; a cup filled with the pinkish liquid that she had been drinking all night. She smiled a little and took the cup, her words of thanks lost into the blaring music.

By the time they were done dancing, it was two in the morning and the harsh fluorescent lights were turned back on, so that the club would begin to filter out. Jackie was tipsy again—she had downed her drink in a hurry to make sure that none of the security guards would notice the neon green wristband that spelled out that she was underage. She clung onto Andre's arm for support, giggling as they rushed out together into the open street, where the cool night air brushed her burning cheeks. In her phone was a half written text message that she hadn't managed to send Penny: 'Things r goin well I think he wants to—.'

"So where do you live, anyway?" Andre asked Jackie. Her eardrums were still pulsating from the hours of loud music, but at least she could hear him talking now.

"Just a mile or two from here... I live in an on-campus dorm," she said.

"What are you, a freshman?" Andre had to have known she was younger than twenty-one, but how young, she had never exactly let on.

"Yeah, I am. It's fine though," she said casually, her nervousness evident despite the sluggishness of the alcohol. Andre just shrugged.

"Alright, that's cool. You're eighteen?" he asked.

"Yeah, eighteen," Jackie responded. Her nerves were quickly ebbing into relief. "What about you?"

"Twenty-two, just graduated. I have a job, but I'm saving up to move somewhere big, you know, not a college town." His hand was running along her back now, and she knew he must have felt her stiffen in—what could it be—disappointment, even though she hadn't even known him for three hours? "Not leaving anytime soon, though. You want me to take you back to your place?"

Jackie shrugged. Despite being initially worried about staying with him, she hadn't even thought about going back to her dorm room. She could hardly call it home; it was more like a 10x15 box that she had to share with a girl named Dolores, a pasty girl who wasn't even friendly enough to ask her about her day, or to talk to her other than when passing the occasional greeting. "No... I mean, it's not even that late yet. We could hang out some first." She was too tipsy, too giggly to force herself into her room now, alone, where Dolores would be sleeping.

"Sounds good. You want to see my place? I don't want to go wasting my time with such a pretty young lady, now." He winked at her, and she giggled. She had caught glimpses of the flirty language he had been using with her inside; things like "hey sexy," and "you're so fine," and something about her body. Out here in the parking lot where she could hear him clearly, his words pleased her all the more.

"Sure thing. Did you drive here?" she asked. Andre nodded, and led her to a dark blue Mustang with thin golden racing stripes running along the sides. He opened the door for her, and she hopped gleefully in, fumbling with the seat belt. He climbed in the car too, and he put his hand on her warm thigh as he put the car in reverse.

"So, do you come here often?" he asked her, moving his hand only to shift into drive, and then reinstating his position on her thigh. He was rubbing his hand now, up and down, right beneath the hem of her sexy red dress.

"No... first time actually. First time being to any club." Jackie brushed a stray hair out of her face, then started running her hands through her locks as the air conditioner blasted, drying whatever bit of sweat hadn't been mopped up already by the cool outside air. Andre stared at her, his eyes hungry. She looked so innocent now, with the exception of that sultry dress, and the slutty way that she had done her make-up, probably to match her friends.

"Well, I'm glad I was there when you were." He slipped his hand up a little bit higher up her thigh, so that he could run a finger along her underwear. He could tell by the expression on her face, that she was buzzed enough to not be too bothered. She squirmed a little bit, and giggled. "What's so funny?" he asked with a playful smile, without withdrawing.

"Nothing. This situation, I guess. Not in a bad way, just in a funny way." His hand felt rough as he ran it along the outskirts of her underwear, and she could feel a chill run down her spine. She didn't pull away though, other than her awkward squirm. She knew that her words weren't making complete sense now, as they pulled up into an unfamiliar driveway. Instead of trying to explain herself, she shifted gears. "Is this where you live? You have roommates?" she asked, then giggled, as if she found her own questioning to be humorous.

"Yeah and yeah... I only have two other roommates and they're out partying till late, so I doubt they're home." He watched as she nodded comfortably. "Shall we go inside?" Still, she gave him comfortable nods. Andre got out of the car and let her out, so that they could walk together up to his front door.

The inside of his house was set up fairly neatly for what Jackie assumed to be an all-male living environment. The kitchen area had a bar and four bar stools instead of a kitchen table, and there were two comfy looking couches set up around a smaller coffee table, with a large TV mounted against one of the walls.

"This is my joint," he said, as he led her over to the bigger of the two couches. "Over here we have a liquor cabinet. If you'd like, I can pour you another drink, but first you've gotta convince me to not feel sleazy about it."

"Sleazy? Now why would you feel that way?" Jackie asked with a giggle. "I'd be plenty fine with another drink."

"You're not afraid of me taking advantage of you?" Andre asked with a sly smile. "That can happen, you know, to pretty things like you."

"Pfffttttt, I know that. I'm not a baby. And you're not going to take advantage of me. I'd like another drink, please." Despite a slight slur, she spoke with such confidence that Andre grinned and began to mix a drink for her out of fruit punch, rum, and a splash of flavored vodka.

"Alright then, whatever you say. Here you are, princess." She giggled and squirmed a little when he handed her the drink, in a way that hinted at bashfulness more than discomfort. Her hair was tied up now by a hair band that had made its home around her wrist all night. Andre brushed a loose strand away from her neck and brought his face close to hers as she drank, just like it had been on the dance floor. "So," he began. "Would you object if I made a move on you?"

Jackie's heart skipped a beat, and she smiled. Her belly was filled with the warmth of the alcohol, and her head had been spinning on and off for the past half hour.

"I dunno, it depends on the kind of move I guess," she said. Her words were coming out more smoothly and naturally than she had anticipated. A brush of shivery excitement ran through her as Andre started kissing the back of her neck. When she didn't object, and only squirmed a little, he kept going, running his kisses up and down and sliding his rough hands up against her thighs. She turned to return a tender kiss, forcing him to slow down to enjoy her lips, if only for a moment. Jackie remembered her friends talking to her about this moment; about going home with someone for casual sex. The thought had been frightening earlier in the night, but now, with Andre's guidance, it didn't feel as casual as she would have expected. She knew that someone she was never going to see again wouldn't have taken care of her like he had.

Andre was working his hands along her body, slipping his hands up over her clothed breasts and squeezing. He knew that this was the way to loosen girls up; tease them first, starting with the breasts and nipples. Jackie had nicely sized breasts that fit perfectly in the palm of his hands. He had made an investment that was well worthwhile with her, one that had coaxed out his caring touch. He slipped his hand under her shirt, which instead of objection earned him a pleasured whimper. Jackie pressed her body against his, leaving her empty cup on the coffee table. She opened her mouth, sliding her tongue sneakily into his mouth. She tasted like liquor and sticky sweetness, which only fueled his desire. She might have been a club virgin, but he could tell that she'd had sex before. Her whimpers turned into high-pitched moans as he thumbed her nipple, her hand appropriately grabbing his crotch. Andre was excited, but forced himself not to rush the foreplay. He wanted this to be perfect; everything that her drunken little mind had ever dreamed of. She knew what a dick felt like and at this moment she wanted it, but he wanted to make her want it even more.

He wrapped his arm around to her back, so that he could lay her down on the couch. Jackie ran her fingers down to his waist, where she untucked his shirt, and made a sloppy movement to pull it up over his head. Andre helped her out, and in a swift motion he had removed her sexy red dress, leaving her exposed in her zebra print bra and leopard print underwear. He didn't mind that her undergarments didn't match; in fact, he found something adorably playful about it. Still, he wanted them gone. He unbuckled the back of her bra and flung it to the floor, leaving her bare chest exposed, her breasts pointed high in the air as her chest heaved with excitement. She drew her arms back in for a moment, as if to try and cover her chest, but Andre just brushed them away so that he could worship to her breasts, sucking on them, and occasionally nibbling on her nipples.

Jackie writhed underneath him in pleasure. She managed to unbutton Andre's jeans while he fondled her breasts, so that she grabbed at his dick first through his underwear, and then forced her way into the tight space in his pants. She gasped with excitement when she found what she was looking for. Andre's dick was the biggest one she had ever felt width-wise, and upon exploring further she realized that it was generous in length too, and extended well into the leg of his pants. She began to use her legs to push the pants and underwear off, which Andre also facilitated as she kept her hand wrapped around his dick, stroking it.

"How do you like that cock, huh babe?" he asked her with a smug smile.

"God, you're hung," she muttered, pulling him into another kiss. Its sweetness again nearly brought him to a halt, providing a short break from the sexuality stirring in the room. "Your roommates aren't going to come back while we're here, are they?"

"Nah, they won't," Andre said, placing more faith in that than he knew he could afford. Chances were it'd be another hour before they came home from the party they'd been talking about for weeks, the one that they had tried time and time again to get Andre to accompany them to. It was a birthday party for an ex-girlfriend of his, who was still pretty tight with his roommates, but Andre wanted little to do with her. The off chance that people could, however, walk in at any moment amplified the excitement for him, something that he wasn't ready to relinquish.

That's when Andre went down on Jackie. His stubble tickled, but only a little, as he began to run his tongue along her clit, and then down the crease of her cunt. She moaned and twisted as he sucked, feeling like a precious jewel that his tongue was washing over, protecting. She began to thrust against his tongue, her throat echoing with moans of varied pitches. Her thrusting was plenty of indication that she wanted to ride his dick, wanted to feel something thrust back inside her. But he kept tight to his position, trailing his tongue over her clitoris again and again.

"Do you want me to fuck you, or do you want me to make love to you?" Andre whispered, when he finally resurfaced.

"Oh fuck... I don't know..." Jackie panted. "Just do it already. Fuck me... make love to me. Oh fuck... either way, I'm yours."

"Well then..." Andre smirked, and positioned himself. His dick was hard and erect, waiting to test the waters. "Let's see how much you can handle." She spread her legs for him, and he pressed the tip of his dick into her, teasing her for a moment, and then finally pressing into her. Jackie moaned as he began to insert himself, slowly at first to get a feel for being inside her. He thumbed her nipple again as he did so, to keep her wet enough to fit. He pressed into her; he could feel her insides rippling against him as she gasped. He took a deep breath. She was so tight around him, making him want to go faster and faster.

Finally he couldn't hold back anymore. He started thrusting into her and increasing his speed, diving as deep as he could go, as Jackie shrieked with pleasure. He kept massaging her breasts, arching his back and sucking on them occasionally as he pounded into her. They went faster and faster, until Andre was grunting with pleasure. "Oh god, you're so sexy babe. You like it when I fuck you? You like being sobered up by my big dick?"

"Yes, yes, yes!" Jackie shrieked. She could feel an orgasm coming on. Then her whole body began contracting, and she tightened around his dick, her nails gripping into his back so hard she left marks.

Andre couldn't take it anymore; he moaned and pulled out, and pressed his dick to Jackie's lips, which she opened to let him in. She felt his dick throb as warm cum filled her mouth, and when he pulled away from her she swallowed. Andre moved Jackie over a little bit, and slumped down beside her on the couch, where they lay spooning, his still-hard cock pressed against her smooth behind. He wrapped his strong arms against her and kissed the back of her neck. She grabbed his right arm and held it close to her as her eyelids fluttered shut, still grinning faintly.

They lay there for a few minutes, before Andre began to hear voices outside. Jackie hadn't stirred; in fact he was pretty sure that she had passed out. He pulled himself up off the couch and lifted her sleeping figure up into his arms.

"What is it?" she murmured, wrapping her arms around his neck.

"Roommates are home. Don't worry, they won't even know we're here." Except for the clothes that he hadn't gathered, he realized. As the key turned in the lock, Andre pushed his bedroom door shut, and lay Jackie down on his soft bed, already forming a plan to get the clothes and take her home in the morning. He'd be sure to wake up early to sneak his number into her phone.

8 A BIRTHDAY TO REMEMBER

It was the last birthday Derek would have in college. He was turning twenty-two today, and it was his senior year, right before graduation and summer and everyone moving on to bigger and better things. That's what they were told would happen, anyway. But Derek didn't want to graduate. He wanted to stay here with his frat brothers, in their big house with a pool out back that made all the other frat houses jealous. Still, he tried to concentrate on the birthday splendor and the joys of being 22 as he walked back from class to his car.

"Yo, birthday man!" Derek looked up to see a tall man with sandy blond hair waving at him from the bus stop. His arm was moving back and forth in swift, full motion, and when Derek caught his eye, the man gave him a lopsided grin, and started jogging toward him. "Wait up!"

"Chill dude, I'm waiting," Derek said with a laugh. The other man was his friend Austin, who had been his roommate since freshman year, when they met by chance via the random room signup system. They were frat brothers now, and had become best friends after Derek had finally learned to deal with Austin's messy habits.

"Thanks man. Are you heading home?" Austin asked, wiping a few beads of sweat off his forehead with a swift rub of his wrist.

"Yeah, I think so. Need a lift?" Derek asked.

"Ah, sweet, that'd be awesome. Hey man, you're going to love your party tonight. I guarantee it. It'll probably be the best one we've ever pulled," Austin said with a grin.

Derek laughed slightly and began walking again in the direction of his car. "Oh, you don't have to do that, man. Really, no worries."

"Dude, don't be crazy, you know we love that shit! Everyone's invited, and the other guys are all hyped up about it now. Besides, yours is the last party of the year before half the house graduates, so we'd better make it a good one, huh?" Austin punched Derek's shoulder playfully, and Derek chuckled a little, trying to fight the sinking feeling in his stomach as he thought about his looming graduation.

"Well I'm looking forward to it. Did you invite Caroline?" Derek asked. Caroline was his ex-girlfriend from the year before, who had broken up with him before she went to study abroad in France. She was back now, and supposedly had a new French boy that she had brought back with her, who was a year older than her and looking to attend graduate school in the US.

"Well, yeah, we invited her whole sorority, sorry dude. But hey, if it bothers you I'll ask the other girls not to invite her," Austin said quickly. Derek shook his head. His stomach tightened at the thought of seeing her again, but he pushed it away.

"Nah, that's all right. Then none of the other girls will come either. I know you want Tracy to be there, so yeah." He finished his sentence right as they got to Derek's red Ford Fusion. He clicked the key to unlock it, and then he and Austin clambered in, and blasted on the radio and the air conditioning.

"Well thanks man, I appreciate it," Austin shouted over the music. Austin had been interested in Tracy for a few months now, and she showed some promise of reciprocating his interest. She wasn't best friends with Caroline, but she was her housemate, and the girls had rules against excluding only one member as long as they were all good friends. "We have a big surprise for you, too," Austin added.

"Really? Can't wait," Derek shouted back with a grin as he began jamming to the music, daydreaming about his party tonight and wondering who would be there, and what the big surprise could possibly be.

Derek spent the rest of the day in the frat house, playing Call of Duty with Austin and then going in the pool with Josh, his girlfriend Amy, and some of her other friends. By the time he got out of the shower, a few of the guys had hung banners that said "HAPPY BIRTHDAY FUCKER" in the kitchen, and had taped his door shut (as was usually the tradition to do before the birthday boy woke up, but nobody wanted to wake up at 8:00 a.m. on a Friday morning to do it). Some of the girls who generally hung around the house hugged him and wished him happy birthday, and told him that his clean hair smelled good.

Then at last it was 10:00 p.m., and it was time to party. There were two beer pong tables set up outside. The kitchen counter was lined with drinks, and a jug full of Peter's special Blue Juice, next to Austin's deadly Jell-O shots.

"Do you think she'll come?" Derek asked Austin as they each grabbed a Jell-O shot, one blue one and one orange one.

"Who?" Austin replied.

"Caroline," Derek said. "Do you think she'll come to the party?"

"Relax, man, I thought you were over that," Austin answered with a frown.

"I mean, I'm not saying I'm not, I'm just wondering," Derek said roughly. He was a bit irked by Austin's reaction. But it wasn't Austin's fault. It had been a year now; he should have gotten over that long ago. He thought he had, but the thought of her being here forced him to realize how uncomfortable the idea of Caroline still made him.

"I know, I know. But forget about her, man. I know for a fact that someone even better is coming." Austin grinned, and grabbed another Jell-O shot. "Seriously dude, we'd better swallow this shit fast before this party gets crazy and they're all gone."

"They're not going to be gone, you made thousands of these. But seriously, what do you mean someone better?"

"You'll see." Austin laughed, his face twisting into a withholding smirk. "I'd better go check on the beer pong. Josh and Chris are playing now, and I bet $10 on Chris winning. WOOHOO, GO CHRIS!" Austin screamed, as he leapt away.

Derek didn't get to have much time alone after Austin pulled away. Almost immediately, girls started coming up to him, screaming his name, or just hugging him from behind and screaming happy birthday wishes into his ear over the loud base. The DJ started up, and the inside of the house was hardly the atmosphere for conversation. A few of his other friends would come up and high five him, or demand to take birthday shots with him, which he obliged.

The night was becoming a whirlwind of dancing and drinking, a dizzy mix of colors and lights and sounds. And Derek was happy, as thoughts of graduation and Caroline began to seem increasingly insignificant, under the sweet influence of alcohol. It was his birthday, and he was going to party like that was all there ever was. The house was packed and at least one person had fallen in the pool by the time Austin hit Derek with his big surprise.

"MAKE WAY!" Austin shouted, as two muscular men that Derek had never seen before carted out a platform with a giant cake.

"Dude, what the fuck!" Derek laughed, shoving his friend Josh playfully as he grinned in awe at the cake. "This shit is legit! That's the biggest cake I've ever seen!" Derek had never even been to a party of this size that had had a cake. And in a moment of drunken emotion, his throat felt dry, like it was swelling up with all that emotion, and for a moment before he recuperated, he simply couldn't speak. One of the girls started out a drunkenly sung "Happy Birthday To Derek" that died down when her voice faded away into drunken sways and giggles.

That's when the cake moved.

The cake was moving, and not because of the platform it was on. It looked alive, like something was moving inside of it. Derek hardly had any time to think about that, because a second later, out of the top of the cake exploded a beautiful woman, wearing nothing from the waist up. She had cake frosting on top of her perky tan breasts, enough that it just managed to cover each of her nipples. Derek wasn't sure if she had planned it like that or if it had just been a coincidence. Her blonde hair looked so smooth, as if she had never actually popped out of the cake at all. The woman threw her hands up in the air, and called out, "Happy Birthday, Derek! Where's the birthday boy?" She looked around with a small smile, her dark eyes dancing in the light of the party.

"He's over there!" came a shout.

"RIGHT HERE!" Josh was standing closest to him out of all his frat brothers, and pointed his big hammy fingers above Derek's head, gesturing wildly to catch the woman's attention.

"Well all right, let's get this party started," said the woman, and a roar of cheers rose from the half of the party that was watching. Derek watched, dumbfounded as the woman rose the rest of the way out of the cake, gyrating her frosting-covered hips as she did so. She had long legs that were a warm, sun-kissed color like her breasts. She was wearing only a pair of underwear, which was almost entirely drenched in icing. She lifted herself the rest of the way out of the cake, and then started walking toward Derek, swinging those frosting-covered hips.

"Have a seat, birthday boy," she said as she approached him. One of Derek's friends pushed him back into a chair that hadn't been there before, or maybe it had and he just hadn't noticed it. He was too enthralled with the woman who had come out of the cake.

The woman so close now, Derek could have reached out and touched her. But there was no need, because she turned around now, so that her supple, rounded ass was facing him. And then she began to dance, gyrating those hips again, so that her ass moved and moved, slowly then quickly, gracefully like a dancing snake. The crowd went wild, and several guys were staring in such awe that it gave some sneaky pranksters the opportunity to push them into the pool.

And then the woman pulled herself onto Derek's lap, where she continued to dance, teasingly. Was this a birthday stripper? She hardly had anything more to take off. Unless...

The woman slid a finger along her breast, wiping the cake frosting off of her perfectly round nipple. She slid her fingernails against Derek's mouth and offered him the frosting. Derek opened his mouth a little bit, as the crowd cheered wildly. He closed his eyes as he sucked the frosting off of her finger, as his drunken sensations blurred together into a haze, flipping wildly in his mind.

The woman took her finger back and winked at him, then continued dancing. He waited for her to offer him another taste of the frosting, but she didn't, she just kept on dancing. And when she was done, she threw her hands up into the air and headed back toward the platform, leaving him with only the mark of her lipstick on his cheek.

Derek wanted to react. He wanted to jump up, to call the woman back to him. He wanted to ask her what her name was, and whether she was interested in coming back to the party with him. She must've been a professional, though, and professionals hardly ever stayed at parties.

But the birthday shots and booze kept his confidence up. He stumbled out of the chair, but the woman was gone. She must have returned to her platform, no, beyond that, because he could see her from here. She was walking away with the two strong men that she came in with.

"Hey! Wait up!" Derek cried, loudly enough to make the woman and both the strong men accompanying her turn their heads. She stopped walking long enough for him to catch up.

"What's up, birthday boy?" she asked.

"I... I never asked you what your name was," Derek slurred drunkenly. He could feel his arousal returning just looking at her, still nearly naked, with the cake frosting on one nipple.

"My name's Monica," the woman said with a small smile.

"Awesome. Do you go to school here, Monica?" Derek asked, savoring the sound of her name on his lips.

"Not here, but I am a college girl," Monica said with a wink. She turned to walk away again, and the muscular men turned to go with her.

"Would you want to attend a college party with some college guys?" Derek asked her with a smile. "I know you might not do that a lot, but I'd really like to get you a drink."

"A drink? How considerate of you," Monica said with a laugh. "I guess I can stay for a drink. You're our only party of the night. As long as my buddies can stay too, of course," she gestured back at the two muscular men who she had been with the whole time. They were both bald and tall, and neither of them looked like they could be her boyfriends. Who would cart her around their girlfriend to these events and watch as she gave birthday lap dances while practically naked?

"Yeah, sure," Derek said, grinning with disbelief.

"Do you mind if you grab it while I look around? It's a pretty sweet place you got here," Monica said, batting her lashes.

"Absolutely," Derek replied, and then headed off toward the drink table, where he sloppily poured out two cups of the Blue Juice. He fought his way back to where he had left her. There stood the two muscular men, but Monica was off somewhere in the party, nowhere to be found.

For a moment he imagined that he was so drunk that he had fabricated her in his mind. Then he shook his head, sobering up just a tiny bit, and headed off into the crowd, determined to find her.

Derek found Monica right when he had almost given up: she was in his bedroom, sprawled across his neatly made bed. She had cleaned the cake off of her breasts since he had last seen her, and she lay in only her underwear. Her large hips sank into his bed, and her breasts were pointed high in the air, like flags, signaling him over.

"How'd you know this was my room?" Derek asked. He was dumbfounded by just what a stupid question that was for a moment like this, and cursed himself out in his head. Monica, however, just laughed.

"I have my ways," she said with a wink. Derek nodded, transfixed by her voice, her body language. She was a sexual machine, waiting to come and take care of him. There was no denying her interest, the way she was poised now, like a tigress waiting to pounce.

"Do you now?" Derek said. He began to advance upon her. His tongue felt heavy, but his libido rose sky high, consuming him as he ran his eyes to where her body met the bed. "Tell me more about these ways."

"Well, for starters, I always get what I want," Monica purred, kicking her legs back playfully. She seemed even more mysterious and seductive now than she had while dancing for him. She had actually taken an interest in him, despite the fact she only came here with the intention of earning some bucks.

"Always? Is that so?" Derek smirked, his confidence and pride soaring as his erection grew. "What kinds of things do you want right now?" He was closer to her now, his face hovering over her neck as he crawled onto the bed. He brushed his lips across her hair, and then trailed down back to her neck, which he bit playfully.

"I think you can figure it out," she said with a low laugh. "You seem like a smart enough boy." She reached over and ran a hand through his hair, then pulled his head toward hers. She kissed his lips tenderly at first, then with tongue, biting his lower lip gently to reaffirm her arousal and willingness.

"I guess that's me," he whispered. He kissed her back and grabbed her body, and pulled her body close to him. He drunkenly removed his T-shirt with a few movements of his strong right arm. He could feel her breasts pressing against his warm, exposed chest now. He moved down to kiss them, to lick them. They still tasted like frosting, with a subtle hint of sticky sweetness to them. Monica threw back her head and sighed in ecstasy as he touched her, her movements growing more and more intense. He could tell that she was a woman with sensitive breasts just like Caroline had been; a woman who would move at the slightest touch, moaning constantly at the sexiest pitches.

"I'm not here to play coy though, so I'll tell you exactly what I'd like," Monica whispered breathily. "I'd like you to fuck me, right here, right now."

"I think we can work that out," Derek said with a smile. He wrapped his fingers around her panties and slid them down, off of her legs. The fabric felt warm and sticky, just like her breasts. But this wasn't remnants of the cake; everything she did spelled out arousal, and this was one of the clearest signs yet that she was ready. He slid a finger along her vaginal opening just in case, stroking her clit and then inserting his finger into her wet pussy. He couldn't resist testing the waters, and now he couldn't put off fucking her for any longer.

He sat her up and guided her so that she was just above his lap, facing away from her, with his dick erect and bulging against his underwear. He removed his pants and his underwear even more quickly than he had removed his shirt, and then guided her down onto his hard cock.

Monica moaned as Derek's dick filled her up and closed her eyes, biting her own lip slightly so as to quiet herself. "God fucking damn it," she sighed, and that's when she started to take control, to move faster, up and down on his dick. Derek reached around to her front and grabbed her breasts, squeezing them and inciting another ecstatic moan. It felt so good the way she was riding him, as if she were the most experienced cowgirl he'd ever met.

"God, you're so tight," Derek grunted with pleasure. She laughed breathily, and continued to ride up and down his dick, touching his nipples every so often and moaning louder and louder each time. Then she stared him straight in the eyes.

"Keep talking dirty to me," she said. Her

eyes, her thrusts were hungry for more, and Derek knew that only a crazy good fucking could bring her satiation.

"Get over here," Derek hissed aggressively. He lifted her up again, forcefully shifting her onto her hands and knees so he could control how fast he fucked her. "You've been a tease all night and now I'm finally going to have everything I want." He inserted himself into her again, and then began to fuck her from behind, harder than she had been capable of fucking him. She knew he was in control now, and he reached over to put his hand to cover her mouth as she shrieked with pleasure. "Don't be too loud... You've been a bad girl," he said as he slammed into her.

"Oh god, I'm cumming!" Monica started gasping for air, her muscles contracting violently. He could feel her tightening around his dick, and he tried his best to hang in there for just a moment longer.

"Holy shit, holy shit," Derek panted as he picked up speed for the last time. Monica was shrieking now, unable to be discrete. He reached forward and grabbed a breast again, and then pulled out just in time to cum all over her back. He gasped and closed his eyes as Monica's body slumped with a final moan. She held still, as the semen dripped down her and pooled in the perfect nook where her lower back met her ass. He collapsed into his bed, and reached for the side table for a couple of tissues to help her clean herself off.

"Was that worth the wait?" Monica asked, her breathing still heavy.

"I'd say so. Was it worth staying here?" Derek asked, grinning now.

"I'd say so too," Monica said with a wink. "Congratulations, birthday boy. Consider yourself special. I don't do this very often, and I dance at a lot of birthday parties."

"I'm flattered," Derek said, his grin growing even goofier. "Why me, anyway?"

"I dunno. I guess you're my type, and I was feeling pretty turned on. I really dig your hair, and you have a nice face. I guess it worked out well," she said happily.

"I couldn't agree more," Derek mumbled, his eyes slowly starting to shut. He was grinning sleepily as her words echoed inside his head. Nothing could bother him now; not graduation, not even Caroline. "Happy birthday to me, I guess."

"Happy birthday to you," Monica said in a soft, melodious voice.

9 THE DIRTIEST LIBRARY IN THE WORLD

Ariana was proud of her school's library. It was one of the biggest in the country among public universities, and she had opted to volunteer there for the past two years as an assistant to the head librarian. She helped organize the books that students left out of order, took some classes on tours through the rows and rows of shelves, and taught all of her friends how to understand the Dewy Decimal System.

Ariana was a slender young girl with a small frame and sleek blonde hair she kept pulled back in a French braid against her neck. She didn't wear glasses like the typical description of a bookworm would suggest; she prided herself on being able to read each and every word in any sized print without help.

Today started out as a day like any other. She was at the checkout counter, going through files on the computer when a male student came up to her.

"Hey, can you help me find a book?" he asked. Ariana looked up to see a tall boy with chestnut brown hair that curled at the tips. He had green eyes that were gazing earnestly at her, as if there was a sense of urgency behind his request.

"Absolutely. What're you looking for?" Ariana asked.

"The Dirtiest Library on Earth," the boy replied. Ariana frowned slightly, wondering if this was a joke.

"Who's it by?" she asked.

"I don't know," he answered. Ariana looked up at his face, studying it for any hint of a smile, or any other sign that he might have been joking. Nothing. Just those eager eyes. She sighed, and typed the title into the computer, wondering if something would actually come up. When it did, she frowned at the number, trying to decipher where in the library such a strange title would find itself.

"Oh, alright. Follow me," she said. She led the boy to the fourth floor of the library, all the way to the back, frequently checking the numbers on the shelves to guide her. This was a part of the library that Ariana had never found herself in before. The library was far too big for a college girl to have ever seen the whole thing, but somehow the fact still surprised her. Very rarely did people want to actually check out books that were somewhere different.

"Wow, I had no idea this place was so big," said the boy. His green eyes were shadowed now, as the lighting gradually shifted. The deeper in they walked, the dimmer it got. Ariana made a mental note to ask somebody about that.

"Yeah, it's kind of easy to get lost, unless you know your Dewey Decimal System," she said casually. The boy laughed.

"I can't say I'm any good at math," he said. "I'm Rich, by the way."

"Oh. Well, that's good for you, I suppose," Ariana said awkwardly. She continued scanning the numbers on the spines of the books.

"No, I mean that's my name: Rich. I was named after my grandpa. You could call me Richard, but it's too old fashioned," said the boy.

"Oh. Well alright," Ariana said, her cheeks burning with the embarrassment of her social misstep.

"So, you got a name?" Rich asked. Ariana kept her eyes on the books, as she struggled to recover from her self-consciousness. She usually didn't engage in small talk with other students while working here; she found it silly, forgettable. But this was the first time anyone had actually introduced himself to her, or asked for her name.

"Ariana," she said.

"Alright, cool. I take it you like books then?" Rich asked.

"Very much so," Ariana said. "All kinds of books: Gothic, contemporary, poetry, sentimental fiction, you name it." She loved books and this library so much that sometimes she forgot how else to define herself. She was every character she'd ever read about; she would find herself feeling like Jane after a session with Jane Eyre, or like Marie Antoinette after reading one of her extensive biographies. The stories inside the library gave her excitement, made her feel free, even when she felt cooped up among the shelves. Every book was like a trapdoor to another world, a world of excitement or tragedy, political turmoil or love. They all had meaning in their existence, and Ariana knew that even if nobody else could appreciate that, she would, even if it was at the cost of her relationships, and sometimes even friendships.

"Pretty cool," Rich said. Ariana nodded, running her slender fingers along the spines of the books until she found exactly the number she had been searching for.

"Here you are." She pulled the book out and placed it in his hands, but not before she noticed the image on the cover. It was a black and white image of a girl in a man's arms; they were both shirtless and surrounded by shelves of books. Her breasts were pressed against his chest, and there was a look of longing and ecstasy on her face. It was Rich's laugh that pulled Ariana back away from the book and into the real world.

"You look like you don't get a lot of people asking for these books, huh?" the boy asked.

"No, not really," Ariana said, looking at the shelves. This was a college library; she had no idea that those even had erotica in them. As far as she knew, college kids were supposed to watch porn, not read books. Especially boys like Rich. But then again, what did she really know about other college kids, or Rich? She kept her eyes on the books, on the spines with titles that read A Night To Remember, Sex in the Park, and The Woman in White.

"Well, thanks for helping me out," said Rich. "I'll see you around." He smiled at her, and her heart started racing as she smiled back, unmoving. Before she left, Ariana tentatively took the last copy of The Dirtiest Library in the World off of the shelf.

Ariana couldn't check this book out; she didn't want her pristine checkout history tainted by something like The Dirtiest Library in the World. It wasn't that she thought anybody would see that or care, but something inside of her made it feel so wrong. Instead, she grabbed the book cover off of her personal copy of one of her favorites: Rome: a Great Empire, and placed it over The Dirtiest Library in the World. They were about the same size, and although she noticed that The Dirtiest Library in the World was a hundred pages skinnier when it didn't fit perfectly.

This unnecessary sneakiness made her feel even dirtier than if she'd checked it out, but Ariana didn't mind. It was sort of exciting; a nice break from her day to day mundanity. She felt like a leading lady; like she was taking action for once, and like this would be a marker in her own story.

Sitting back behind the circulation desk, Ariana put the book on her legs and flipped it open. She flipped to a page in the middle and read: "I touched him slowly; his dick was warm and familiar in my hand."

Ariana took a deep breath. She shifted positions in her seat, and slipped her hand into her skirt. Succumbing to sudden temptation, she thumbed at her underwear and ran her fingers down to brush against her labia. Ariana shivered and pulled back. She looked around, but nobody was approaching her desk. She was hidden after all; the skirt she was wearing was long, and didn't look like anything was going on underneath it. She kept reading.

"He responded with a swift gesture; his hand firmly cupped my breast. I moaned and he put his hand to my mouth, stifling the sound. He told me to be quiet, that this was the library after all, and we couldn't afford to get caught."

Ariana shivered. She closed her eyes and began to rub against her clitoris. She couldn't believe she was doing this here, out of all places. She inhaled sharply, and slowly slipped the tip of her pointer finger into her vagina. She left it there for a moment. Still nobody was coming toward her. The library had reached its slow hours, and the desk was all hers.

She slipped the finger in further, and took a deep breath. She read the next line.

"I could hardly even manage a 'yes,' I just did what I was told. He picked me up and pushed my body against a shelf, massaging my breasts again." Ariana shivered. Anyone could see her at any moment. Someone could find out, and say things about her. She was rubbing her clitoris now, faster and faster. She pushed her finger in deeper and she gasped as she started to come on her own finger.

"Shit, fuck," she whispered under her breath. She was sitting, so she couldn't push her finger in and out like she could have had she been lying down. She held her breath and imagined that her finger was something more as she continued to read.

"He began to push himself in, slowly at first, but then a power seemed to overcome him, and he began pushing into me more and more quickly."

"You're good to go home."

Ariana jumped at the sound of the voice, and yanked her hand back. Standing in front of her was her supervisor, a tall blonde woman, holding a book in her arms. Ariana nodded and grabbed her book, then jumped out of her seat and straightened her skirt. Her heart was still pounding by the time she reached the street.

By the next day Ariana had finished the book. She slipped it back on the shelf in the morning before class, before anyone could notice the little empty place from where she had taken it. As if anyone would have noticed. She liked the feeling of sneaking around the library in the wee hours of the morning, when the only people there were kids who had pulled all-nighters studying or writing papers. They were all too tired to care to notice her anyway.

"I didn't expect to see you here." Ariana spun around and saw Rich standing behind her. He was smiling, and his eyes had what almost looked like a light humor to them.

"Here as in the library? Then you must've confused me with someone else... I'm here all the time," Ariana said quickly.

"This section of the library," Rich corrected. "You seemed really taken aback yesterday."

"Well, I'm just doing my research," Ariana snapped, annoyed that she had seemed so uncomfortable before. She didn't want to be taken as some naïve little girl, who was unaware that sex even existed.

"Are you?" Rich raised an eyebrow. "Interesting."

"Whatever. You're only allowed to check out one book at a time, I don't know why you're here," Ariana said. She couldn't bring herself to take the bitter edge out of her voice.

"I know. I just returned the book I

checked out yesterday. And I got here early to see if I could check out another with a title that's more school-appropriate," Rich said.

"You read often?" she asked, doubtful that he was telling the truth. Then again, what benefit would lying have?

"I'd say so. I have a pretty big personal library, not to brag or anything," he said with a laugh. Ariana recognized the statement as a quote from the book, and her cheeks grew warm.

"How big is it?" she demanded, before she could stop herself. It was the follow-up quote from the book. She wasn't sure if he'd pick up on it, but she was dying to let him know that she wasn't the prude baby that he seemed to unjustly think she was.

"You wanna see it?" Rich asked. Even in the dim lighting of the Erotica section, Ariana could see that the intensity in his eyes paralleled the same intensity she had noticed on the first day they had spoken. This was unscripted; the conversation that Ariana had read in The Dirtiest Library in the World had gone on for longer, with more innuendos. It wasn't until later on that the sex had happened.

"Sure," Ariana blurted, before she could stop herself. Her voice was smoother now, paralleling what she imagined scenarios like this should be like. Rich grinned. In the little bit of time that they had spent together, she hadn't noticed how nice his smile was.

"Follow me," he said, before disappearing behind the shelves.

Ariana was surprised when he led her out of the library and into the parking lot, where he stopped at a blue Lexus.

"Sorry it's a mess. Hop on in," he said, opening the door for her. Ariana paused, nervous at first, then forced herself in. It was what heroines always did anyway; they were active characters, and she had spent too much of her life being passive.

"Where're we going?" she asked.

"I told you, I'm going to show you my library," he said, grinning again. His expression seemed so playful, so casual, and put Ariana at ease. Still, she was nervous. She wasn't sure if they were still speaking in innuendoes, or where he was actually going to take her. She had completely forgotten about class and would probably end up missing it, but it was time she took a risk.

"All right. So do you actually like books or are you just a pervert?" she asked. When Rich frowned, she giggled, hoping to convey the more joking tone that she might have failed to represent. His expression softened.

"What's your guess?" he asked.

"Well if you have a large library, you must like to read," she said smoothly. She started to tug her hair free of her French braid, trying to let loose. He laughed.

"Good call," said Rich.

They pulled up in front of a house after less than ten minutes. It was small, with a yellow paint job and a blue roof, shaded behind some palm trees. Ariana straightened her skirt and walked to the door with Rich, holding her bag at her side like a lady. She followed him inside, not sure of what to expect.

"It's just my two roommates and I that live here... we have a fourth room and, well, lemme show you," Rich said. He led her through the living room and to a room that had double doors, a surprisingly nice touch for a college house. "After you," he said, pulling them open for her.

"Oh my..." Ariana gasped. The room had bookshelf upon bookshelf lining the walls. The only space that wasn't covered was where windows had been placed. And even there, smaller bookshelves lay underneath the windows. There were old books with beat up spines and faded colors, and new books that were shining in the sun, as if they had never been handled before.

"Hopefully this answers your question from before," Rich said. He was watching her with that smile of his, his eyes boring into her.

"Absolutely. You really do have a huge library," she breathed. She had to admit, she was turned on. She had never met a boy, friend or otherwise, who had cared to have his own library, who loved reading so much - he even read erotica.

"You know it," Rich said. "Now how about I show you my dick?"

"Your dick?" Ariana asked. Even with his little hints, she had never expected the sentence to be delivered in such a way.

"You know it's what we've been jumping around this whole time," Rich said. His whole face said that he wanted her: the way he was staring into her, the way he was biting the corner of his lip ever so slightly.

"I suppose you're right," Ariana said. She looked around again and then back at him, greeted by a new wave of arousal. "Would you like me to help you out?"

"Don't mind if you do," Rich said. Ariana nodded and advanced toward him. She grabbed his buckle and tugged it loose. This was it, everything her spontaneity and reckless behavior had led up to. And she wasn't going to turn back now. That wouldn't be the heroine-like thing to do. She began to unbutton his pants and gave them a tug to reveal his forest green underwear.

"Nice color," she said offhandedly.

"Thanks, I don't get that very often," Rich said with a laugh. Ariana felt her cheeks heat up a little. Of course girls who were about to engage in sexy behavior with a guy didn't comment on the color of his underwear; the fit, maybe, but not the color. Now that she thought about it, though, the fit was very nice. She could see the outline of his hard dick clearly, bursting to be freed. With a rush of confidence, she reached over and began to trace her fingers along it. Already hot with arousal, she reached into his underwear and gently grabbed his dick and slipped it out. It was warm in her hands, and even larger than it had looked when inside his underwear. She took a deep breath and began to stroke it with her hands. It had to be at least seven or eight inches long, and it was nice and thick around.

"What do you think?" Rich asked breathily. She could tell he was enjoying himself by the way his eyelids fluttered when she moved her hands up and down, up and down.

"Take a guess," Ariana said with a smirk. Rich didn't answer. Instead, he shoved her against the nearest bookshelf and began to kiss her passionately. Ariana kissed him back, enthralled by a mixture of their environment and the presence of this man before her. She ran her hands along his chest and yanked his shirt off over his head. He pulled her blouse off smoothly, revealing her perky breasts, held back by a lacy white bra. He ran his lips down her neck, kissing her all the way down to her collar bone, and then her breasts. Ariana shuddered; she could feel her heart pounding, her nipples growing hard at his touch.

"I want to fuck you so badly," Rich whispered. Ariana could feel his erection pressing up against her, and her body going weak. She smiled and began to pull his pants and underwear down the rest of the way. She knelt to help him tug the pants over his feet when Rich pressed his dick against her face. Ariana instinctively grabbed his dick again and began to jerk him off, then realized what he was hinting at. Barely hesitating, she licked the tip of his dick slowly, then wrapped her lips around it and slid it into her mouth. Rich gasped and began to fuck her mouth slowly, thrusting his length in and out of her mouth. Then, he pulled her to her feet. "Over here."

Rich led her over to a soft bench covered in velvet that sat at the foot of one of the shelves. Ariana could feel her heart pounding as he lay her down; she was among so many books, with the hottest man she had ever had the pleasure of sleeping with.

"I'm about to rock your world," he whispered as he unfastened her bra.

Ariana's breasts were finally exposed to the cool air now. Rich leaned over to kiss her chest, stroking her nipples carefully until they were both fully swollen with desire. She moaned and her back arched, pushing against the soft chair. Rich moved to slip off her black skirt, leaving her in just her lacy white underwear. He smiled with satisfaction, admiring his work. Then he turned and kissed her nipples tenderly, running his tongue along their surface. Ariana gasped, and wrapped her arms around his neck. He continued moving, until he was on top of her.

Without asking her if she was ready, he pressed his dick against her pussy and began to push himself into her. Ariana gasped; of course she was ready. She spread her legs for him and he grabbed them, lifting them over her head. He had done this before, she could tell. He knew just the way he had to hold her to give her maximum pleasure. She moaned as he pushed himself into her; she was nice and wet, so he slid in easily despite his size.

"Oh God," Ariana moaned. She was digging her nails into his back now; she couldn't help it as he sped up and began to thrust into her, faster and faster. He held her in her position; she couldn't move even if she wanted to. But he felt so good inside of her, unlike anything she had ever experienced before. This wasn't boring like the last time she'd had sex; it was anything but.

"Fuck," Rich muttered. His eyes were closed as he fucked her. If she arched her head just right, she could see his big dick going into her, wet and glistening from their mutual arousal. As she watched, she felt herself overcome with desire and stimulation. Her breathing began to increase.

"Fuck me harder," she moaned into his ear. Rich didn't delay a moment in delivering. He began to pound into her, and Ariana screamed, her cries echoing through the library. She wondered if Rich's roommates were home and listening to them.

"You like being fucked here? You like feeling swept the fuck away? How do you like making my dick so hard I could fuck you all day?" Rich hissed. Ariana couldn't respond. She could feel her body weakening, giving in to all the pleasure.

She began twitching, but he held her firmly, and he put a hand over her mouth to stifle her loud moans as she came. Rich closed his eyes, breathing heavily. He kept fucking her until he could hardly stand it, and pulled out to cum all over her chest.

Ariana moaned and ran her finger along her breasts. They felt warm and sticky. She closed her eyes and lay there for a moment, relishing in the aftermath of orgasm. She only opened her eyes again when she felt something soft running along her breasts. Rich had pulled a tissue out from seemingly nowhere and was gently wiping her down with it, helping clean up his mess. Ariana couldn't help but smile a little.

"You know John Waters?" she said quietly. She was using her library voice again. "The film director?"

"Yeah, what about him?" Rich asked. He finished up with a second tissue, and was now stroking her smooth skin with his hand.

"Well, he had a quote that goes, 'We need to make books cool again. If you go home with somebody and they don't have books, don't fuck them.' That's been my plan since I heard it a few years back." She laughed to herself. Rich was smiling.

"I'm glad I had enough books to impress you," he said. And then he kissed her lips.

"Me too." She smiled. "After all, this is

the dirtiest library in the world." She laughed at her own cheesy reference to the book. Rich laughed with her.

"I knew you read it. I've been trying to get your attention for a little while now. I don't think that you'd remember; you hardly even look at people's faces when you check books out for them." Rich said.

"Oh. Sorry about that." Ariana smiled sheepishly.

"Don't apologize. You've seen things you won't be able to un-see now," he said with a wink.

"I don't doubt that," Ariana said. They sat in silence for a moment, before she spoke again, a grin crossing her face.

"How about I show you my library?" she said.

10 TEACH ME SOMETHING GOOD

Scott could lose his job. Hell, he could lose his reputation and his job for being here at the same party as a student. That's what his superiors had told him. "We know you're young," they had said. "And we know that you're a student yourself. But this is the graduate level. And if you're going to be teaching undergraduate classes, you absolutely cannot have any relations, consensual or otherwise, with your students. And it goes without saying that you're not allowed to attend parties where your students are present, either."

He knew that such a thing could screw him over in trying to get his master's degree. It would also screw up the budding relationship that he was hoping to have with one of his fellow graduate students, Clara, a young geology student with a heart of gold.

But there she was, Vanessa Gardener from his 10:00 a.m. Short Story class, surrounded by his curious young colleagues. He could hear the questions buzzing around the room. How old was this girl? Who had brought her here? And most importantly, is she in any of our classes? Nobody seemed to know the answer, but Scott knew it didn't matter. He knew that he'd have to leave the party and that would be the end of it. He said goodbye to his close friends, and made a humble beeline for the exit, skirting around her in an attempt to remain unseen, hidden.

"Professor Baxter!" Scott stopped in his tracks when he heard the voice. He forced a smile and turned around.

"Hello Vanessa. Fancy seeing you here." He twiddled his thumbs anxiously, hoping that the exchange would be as brief as he intended it to be. She laughed, a drawn out laugh, one that included tossing her long, dark hair back.

"I don't know if you've met my older brother, AJ? He's the one who brought me here," she said, flashing him a smile as she pointed to a tall, dark-haired man who shared her nose. Scott's stomach dropped uncomfortably at the recognition.

"Oh, AJ. Yeah, we're friends. But you probably already knew that, didn't you?" Scott asked.

"You betcha. I asked him if he knew you when we walked in, and told him you were my teacher," Vanessa said with a wink. She swayed a little; she was clearly tipsy, despite being only twenty or so, since she was a sophomore. He wondered why on earth AJ had brought her here, knowing that she was underage. He probably hadn't known that Scott was her teacher, though, so his intentions must have been good.

"Well, alright then. It was good seeing you, Vanessa. I'm not supposed to be at a party where my students are, so I'm gonna go." He wasn't sure if he intended on making her feel guilty by adding that, but he was a little bit frustrated. He had so much work between graduate school and grading papers for his two classes that he rarely got to go out. And now that he finally had the chance he couldn't stay. He made a mental note to ask AJ to never bring her to another party.

"Aw, don't go because of me. Stay!" Vanessa whined. She was smiling, her lips shining with the sexy lipstick that she had been reapplying since she got here. She leaned in against him for a hug, pushing her large breasts up against him.

Scott felt a rush of lust wash over him,

but pulled back, muttering, "No, I can't."

He hadn't imagined he'd ever be such a sucker for the student-teacher thing, at least not until he'd met Vanessa.

Ever since the first class they'd had together, Vanessa'd had her eye on him. She'd come up after class, told him very slowly in an attractively low voice that she had enjoyed their lesson and that she couldn't wait for the next one. She'd made joking comments about how he was the most attractive teacher she had, and then wink in a way that left him clueless as to whether or not she was coming onto him. He was fairly sure she was, though. She'd shown up at his office hours a few times wearing inappropriately low-cut shirts that drew his eyes down to her large breasts, shirts that no decent young lady should wear out of the house, even on the hottest of days.

It turned him on though, but he would never admit it, or play into her games. He'd taken to sending her away with a quick, sometimes unsatisfactory answer to her question, and a fabricated excuse for office hours being diminished that day.

Now, here she was, playing another one of her games. Pouting up at him for leaving, her eyes ravenous with hunger for him.

"Stay for a drink with me?" she whined. Even when she was tipsy, she managed to keep her physical composure. Her hair was still perfectly straight, her makeup without a single flaw.

"I'm sorry, I can't stay," Scott insisted. "I'll see you in class, Vanessa." With that he forced himself to turn, and walk away from her. However, instead of walking out the door, he turned and headed for AJ. He tapped him on the shoulder, pulling him out of his current conversation. AJ turned, initially confused, and then grinned and pulled Scott into a hug.

"Hey man, what's up?" he asked, his eyes excited, comfortable with the atmosphere.

"Not much. Vanessa's your sister?" Scott asked. He wasn't sure what he was hoping to get from this.

"Uh, yeah. She told me tonight she's in your class. Pretty neat, huh?" AJ said. He adjusted his response when he saw Scott's uncomfortable expression.

"Oh, shit. She's not supposed to be here, is she?" AJ asked. He didn't teach, and Scott knew it wasn't his place to know the rule, or to keep up with whether or not his little sister was in his friend's class. "Sorry man, I didn't know. She was so lonely today. I thought I'd give her something to do."

"Yeah, I know, don't worry about it. I'm just gonna go. But maybe next time, man, let her stay home?" Scott said. AJ nodded.

"Of course," he replied.

"Thanks," Scott said with a little smile. He was about to leave when he turned around, a second thought emerging. "Has your sister said anything to you about me?"

"About you?" AJ asked. He frowned. "No, not really. Not other than what she told me about you being her teacher and all. She asked me if I knew you and I told her yes. She did say that you were a good teacher. That's all," AJ concluded.

"Okay. Thanks. I'll see you later man," Scott said with a nod. With that, he slipped past Vanessa a final time. She gave him a wink on his way out into the sweltering summer night.

Monday came around a few days later, and with it came Scott's office hours. Students rarely came to office hours for a class like this. They would come at the end of the year, when he assigned final essays on a short story of their choice. Sometimes, they would come for the midterm essay, too. But the summer semester was only a quarter of the way through, so office hours were generally reserved for grading short responses.

Every so often, on days like this, Vanessa would also show up, bringing her lipstick-enhanced smile and batting eyelashes. Still, he had never called her out on her behavior, never told her that it was inappropriate and that he could report her. If the charges were troublesome enough for her, she could just as easily twist the story, and tell officials that he had been coming on to her. No, that was not a line that he wanted to cross.

There was a knock at his door, and then it pushed open, as if whoever was behind it didn't care to wait for a response. He looked up, waiting for Vanessa to open the door and enter into his space once again.

But it wasn't Vanessa. Instead, there stood Clara, the geology student that had his interest. He smiled at her, relieved. She was more plain-faced than Vanessa, less curvy, but he didn't care. He liked her. She was smart, interesting, and seemed to like him too.

"Hey you, what a surprise," Scott said with a smile. Clara smiled back at him.

"A good one, I hope. I brought you some cookies." She handed him a small, ruffled bag, still warm from the oven.

"A great one. You made these?" Scott

asked, opening the bag. The warm scent was already taking over his small office. "Wow. There must be five different kinds of cookies in here."

"Six," Clara said with a wink. "But now you know. I can't stay, though. I have to pick up my niece from daycare. But I just wanted to drop by and say hello and give you this and this." She leaned in and gave him a little kiss on the cheek. "Thanks for picking her up last time for me. My sister really appreciated it."

"Oh, don't mention it," Scott said. He was smiling now, barely able to keep himself from grinning foolishly. "I was happy to help. I'd go with you now to say hi to little Becky but, you know, Monday is office hours." He smiled slightly. He meant it, too. Scott didn't particularly mind kids, but Clara's niece Becky was as sweet as she was.

"Well, I guess I'll see you then. We should grab lunch sometime," she said.

"Absolutely! What about tomorrow?" Scott asked. "Sometime between noon and one?"

"Perfect," Clara said. "I'll text you, and we can figure out the specifics." She smiled at him again and left with a little wave. Scott found himself beaming from ear to ear in his chair. He swiveled around in it, just to emphasize his good mood. He was about to get back into the swing of grading papers when there was another knock at his door. He imagined for a moment that Clara had returned.

As if he should be so lucky. There, standing in the doorway, was Vanessa.

Vanessa was smiling and batting her eyelashes just as he'd imagined her. She was a temptress, here to try to seduce him and to see if he'd break.

"Hello, Vanessa. What can I do for you today?" Scott asked calmly. He avoided direct eye contact with her, and instead took to shuffling papers around.

"I just wanted to say I'm sorry about this weekend," Vanessa replied. Scott looked up, confused by the unexpected apology. She smiled at him, glad to have gotten his attention. "I sincerely did not know that you were going to be at the party. I just wanted to have a fun time with my brother. I didn't know you guys were friends." Her eyes were drilling into him now, filled with a sense of genuine apology.

"Oh, that's alright," Scott said, trying to remain professional, but casual. "I met him two years ago. We were in the same graduating class."

"I should've remembered you from his

pictures," Vanessa said. Her voice was delicate and smooth, like a pearl.

"Well, we haven't taken any recent ones together, anyway," Scott admitted. "My hair was longer two years ago."

"Yes it was," Vanessa said. Scott felt a chill run down his spine at the knowledge that she had looked through photo albums from years ago, just to satisfy some curiosity about him. Something about that was incredibly hot, too.

"Is there anything else I can help you with, Vanessa?" Scott asked calmly. "Preferably class related."

"Your office smells nice today, Scott," Vanessa said. Her voice was as calm as his was.

"Thank you. It's cookies. I'd prefer it if you called me Mr. Baxter," Scott said.

"You told us to call you Scott in class," Vanessa said. "You said Mr. Baxter was too formal." Scott cursed himself for his casual teaching strategy.

"Well, I suppose you got me on that one," Scott said. He tried not to lose his composure. It was true he hadn't had sex in almost a year, and her advances turned him on. But at what price?

"Aren't you going to offer me a cookie?" Vanessa said. She gave him a flirtatious smile, as if she was going to blow him a kiss at any moment.

"Oh, I suppose." Scott felt a pang of

guilt as he handed her the small crumpled bag. She reached into it, her painted red nails flashing at him as she grabbed a chocolate chip cookie.

"Thank you." She took a slow bite, filling her mouth and chewing sexily. Scott tried to ignore her by looking at the papers, anything. But there was something fascinating about how she ate the cookie. This girl would be the end of him.

"Was there something I can help you with?" Scott murmured. He took the cookie bag back from her, thinking now about Clara.

"Oh yes. You see, I have this dilemma," Vanessa said. She got out of her seat and began pacing around the office. Every step she made, her high heels made a little tapping noise on the tile floor. Her low-cut shirt revealed her breasts, bouncing slightly. Her skirt was also red, to match her nails, and was tightly tucked around her curvy behind. "I've been interested in you for quite some time now, Scott. But nothing has come of that. Why is that?"

"I—uh—" The forward nature of the question caught Scott off guard. "I'm sorry Vanessa. You're my student. I'd lose my job if I reciprocated."

"But isn't that the fun part?" she laughed. "What if I told you you'd lose your job if you didn't?"

"I beg your pardon?" Scott cried. His heart was pounding faster now. Vanessa was a villain in his mind, a villain here to torture him and tempt him. But nothing was sexier than a good villain.

"Well, I'm always showing up at your office dressed like this: to impress. You don't think your colleagues haven't noticed by now? They could think that we're having sex in here right now, that we've been having an affair. I don't see any reason to think otherwise," Vanessa said.

"My colleagues trust me," Scott said calmly. Suddenly Vanessa started to let out a loud moan. Scott leapt to his feet, a look of horror on his face, and pressed his hand to her mouth to physically stop her. Her lips felt as warm and large as they pressed against his palm. "Okay, I see your point. Stop it."

Vanessa pushed him away with a smirk. "Fine. But only if you let me help you out with that," she said, pointing to the visible erection pressing against Scott's pants.

"Fuck," Scott muttered. He had walked into a trap. He sat back down to hide the erection. "What do you get out of this blackmail and shit? You already have an A."

"I just want you," Vanessa cooed. She slipped out of her heels and advanced toward him, then planted herself in his lap. "And I know you've wanted me, too. I can see it on your face. Feel it in your pants." She began to run a hand through his short, dark hair.

"What about your brother? We're friends, there's a code against that," Scott blurted. His heart was racing now, his breath slowly picking up speed and weight, as her sultry breath brushed against him.

"All the more reason to want it. Let's not fool ourselves, Scott. You want this for the same reason I want this. Because it's wrong to want it. Because it's dangerous. We go through with this, and you're just going to have to trust that I won't tell on you. After all, why would I want to get the hottest teacher in school fired unless he won't give me what I want?"

Scott was losing. He racked his brain for a way out of this, but his thoughts were numb, directed only toward having sex with this girl. "Lock my door," he said firmly.

"My dear Scott," Vanessa said with a smile. "I already locked it on the way in."

Vanessa pressed her lips to his neck without hesitation; her hot breath was closer than ever now. He leaned back, breathing deeply as she kissed him, and ran her tongue along his skin. He wrapped his arms around her, holding her body close to him as she did so. Every effort he had made up until this point had been futile now that this was the final outcome. But they had already started, and there was no stopping now unless he wanted to upset Vanessa.

But who said he wanted to stop? Scott was humping her now; he could feel her warm pussy on his pants through her underwear. She ripped off his shirt, as if it were all she had ever wanted to do, and clung to his strong shoulders, running her hands and lips up and down his smooth chest and nibbling on him from time to time. Scott slid his own hands up her shirt and around the back, so that he could undo the latch on her bra. Her back felt as warm as the rest of her skin, like her skin was as fiery as her will. Vanessa pulled her own shirt off as her bra fell to the floor. She grabbed one of his hands and pressed it to her breast.

"You like?" she purred. Her breasts were as big as she'd made them look, C-cups probably, maybe even D's. They felt so natural though, he was sure they couldn't be implants. His only response was a low growl as he thumbed her nipple, then slid his tongue along the slope of her breast. She moaned, but it was a soft moan this time, one that Scott knew would go unheard. She rocked against his lap, against his erect dick, and Scott knew that more than anything, she wanted to get fucked, and he wanted to fuck her.

He and Clare weren't even officially dating yet, so this wasn't even exactly cheating. The thought reassured him, as he bit her nipple softly, burying his face in her breasts and moving his tongue along one, then the other. He slid his pants up her skirt, hoping to pull her underwear off. But all he found was smooth skin, and her warm, wet opening. She had never been wearing any underwear at all.

Scott shivered with arousal. He ran his fingers along her wet pussy, back and forth. He made sure he went high enough up to rub her clit in the process, but didn't slip his fingers inside of her. Not yet. This was all her fault, and he would make her wait as punishment. Instead, he concentrated on her clit, rubbing it with two fingers in circular motions.

Vanessa moaned. She reached for his pants buckle and undid it, then threw it on the ground. She adjusted her position in his lap just enough to unzip his pants and yank them down. Scott helped a little bit, lifting himself off the chair just slightly enough for Vanessa to pull his underwear down.

She grabbed his dick and began stroking it. She was going slowly, teasing him as much as he was teasing her. This was all another part of Vanessa's game with him. He began to rub against her clit, faster and faster. She moaned softly and jerked him off, her hand sliding faster and faster up and down his dick. But Scott wanted more. He grabbed her, and lifted her up, placing her on his desk on top of his papers. He left her seated, just so they wouldn't knock anything over and cause a commotion.

Scott spread her legs and pushed her skirt up and out of the way. He went down on her, licking her clit and inserting one of his fingers slowly into her. She gasped and leaned back as he ran his tongue up and down, thrusting his finger in and out, in and out. He continued to lick her breasts while he was at it. He licked them at first, touching one nipple at a time with his wet tongue. Then he began to suck on them, biting her nipple softly. They were so big and soft against his mouth, her nipples so hard. Eventually, he pulled her down from the desk.

"If you want to help me with this so badly, why don't you be a good student and suck my dick," Scott said.

"If you insist, professor," Vanessa said

with a smirk. "I thought you'd never ask." She got on her knees as Scott sat back down in the chair, pulling her skirt the rest of the way off. She got to work on sucking his dick. She placed it in her mouth, between those big, red lips, just the tip at first, then as much of it as she could take. Scott moaned as she went up and down, up and down. His dick felt so hard and wet in her mouth. It felt hot like her pussy, which had been so wet when he touched it.

"Keep touching yourself too," he whispered. It was something that he imagined he would enjoy watching. He wasn't wrong about that, either. Vanessa was enjoying herself so much his dick was silencing louder moans. He began to thrust slowly, still letting her do most of the work. His breathing quickened watching her pleasure herself; watching those red finger nails go in and out of her, then up to her clit. They were glistening with wetness, shining with her arousal for him. Scott moaned softly. He could feel her tongue against his dick. But she stopped a moment later, her eyes burning with intensity and desire.

"Fuck me," she said. "Right here, right now."

Scott roughly lifted Vanessa up and into his lap. Only then did he notice how light she was. He grabbed his dick and slowly inserted it into her, causing her to moan with pleasure. Then he started fucking her, still in the sitting position, with her in his lap facing him. Vanessa proved as he'd expected, to be a good top. She loved his dick; she'd been craving it from the first moment she stepped into his class and decided that she was attracted to him. She moved up and down on his dick with ease, fucking him in a way that he could feel himself going all the way inside her. He fucked her back, thrusting up against her and as far into her as he could go. He shuddered with pleasure.

Scott could smell her arousal. He fucked her hard as she went up and down, up and down, at just the right angle to make her nearly scream.

But she couldn't scream, unless they wanted to get caught. Scott placed his hand over her mouth, silencing her as he thrust into her. She had stronger legs than he'd imagined, and she kept moving up and down on his dick, in a seemingly tireless fashion.

But Scott wanted a chance to be in control. "Get up," he grunted. He laid her down under his desk and then got on top of her, doggy style, fucking her from behind. She was still wet, so they resumed easily. Then, he thrust into her with all he had, going faster, faster, faster than he had fucked in a long time. Vanessa had put her own hand against her mouth, her eyes were closed and she was moaning against her own skin, trying desperately to keep quiet. He reached around and held his own hand to her mouth for extra security.

"Quiet, you little slut," he hissed. He wasn't about to get caught, not now. He could feel himself beginning to give way, about to pull out and cum on her, when suddenly he felt Vanessa cum. Her body began to contract, and she began to writhe underneath him, her face spelling out euphoria. He couldn't help himself; he gave a final few thrusts and came too, inside of her. Vanessa's moans were still muffled by his hand, and he kept his hand firmly against her mouth until he finally pulled out, panting. "Shit," Scott muttered.

Vanessa took a moment to respond as she regained her composure, still panting. "Lucky for you I'm on birth control. Nothing will come of that." She said it with such confidence that for a moment Scott almost didn't worry. But he was still nervous. With his semen inside her, Vanessa could easily prove that they'd had sex, or worse, claim that he'd raped her if she wasn't satisfied. He felt his insides clench with anxiety and regret.

Vanessa eyed him and smirked, reading his reaction. "You're still the hottest teacher in school. I'm not letting you out of my sight just yet. You're the hottest fuck in the school too, as far as I've experienced." She began collecting her clothes, sliding her bra on first, then her low-cut shirt. He wondered what she meant by not letting him out of her sight. Was it a threat that this would happen again, or maybe she just meant to reassure him that she wouldn't let him get fired?

"I'll see you in class," Scott said, trying to keep whatever sexy, teacher confidence he had. Vanessa winked at him, appearing to be not at all dissatisfied. She pulled a comb out of her purse to tame her hair, still breathing more heavily than usual, clearly still aroused from the sex.

"You too, Professor Scott," she said as she put her comb away. She brushed off her clothes then walked out, slowly, just to give him time to watch her from behind as she sauntered out. Once she had left, Scott peered out into the hall. There was no indication of life, or that anybody could have possibly heard them.

With worrisome thoughts diminishing, Scott couldn't say that he'd regretted the experience. In fact, thinking about it still turned him on. He sighed with relief, packed his papers into his briefcase, and checked his phone as he headed out. On the screen was one new text message from Clare: Lunch, 12:30, Blue Jay Café. See you there.

AUTHOR'S NOTE

Readers: I want to expand a few of the stories to see where the characters can be explored further. If there are any of the stories that you would like to read more about again, I'd love to hear from you!

Visit my blog at www.sageyarber.com

Join my newsletter for free exclusive previews
www.sageyarber.com/in

Follow me on Twitter at
www.twitter.com/sageyarber

Like my page on Facebook at
www.facebook.com/sageyarber

Discover my books at major ebook retailers everywhere.